'From No...
Fi...

They don't need...

'Perfectly,' she replied, her voice ...

'Good,' he said, turning on his heels and marching back to the truck. He couldn't recall ever being so fired up at someone. Then again he'd never had a woman get under his skin like Amanda Lucas.

'Women,' he said, with a shake of his head. 'Who needs 'em?'

The only answer he got was an immediate tightening in his chest.

When he got to his truck, he glanced back and saw that Amanda was still standing in the spot where he'd left her. It looked as though her eyes were glistening with tears. But he couldn't be sure.

Climbing behind the wheel he wondered if he'd done the right thing by telling Amanda to stay away from his girls. She clearly loved them, and he knew they were crazy about her.

Of course he'd been right, he told himself a moment later.

The problem was, could *he* stay away from her?

Dear Reader

As November brings cold days and dark nights, what better way to spend your time than curled up indoors reading our fantastic Desire™ line-up!

Firstly, welcome back top author Ann Major who brings us our **Man of the Month**, sizzlingly sexy film star, Joey Fasano. And then meet two irresistible cop heroes. Andy Gautier is called upon to investigate a woman's mysterious memory loss in *Her Holiday Secret* by Jennifer Greene. And Marie Ferrarella brings us the latest instalment in her Cutler family saga where Sheriff Quint Cutler puts his future wife in jail!

Everybody's looking for a missing pregnant woman in our **Follow That Baby** cross-line mini-series which continues this month with *The Daddy and the Baby Doctor*. Don't miss the next two instalments in December and January, also in Desire, and then the exciting conclusion in February in the Sensation™ series!

Finally, to round off this month's line-up, enjoy a delightful baby story from Christy Lockhart and envy Pamela Macaluso's lucky heroine who's sheltered from a storm by a handsome stranger.

Happy reading!

The Editors

The Daddy and the Baby Doctor

KRISTIN MORGAN

SILHOUETTE
DESIRE

*Silhouette, Silhouette Desire and Colophon
are registered trademarks of Harlequin Books S.A.,
used under licence.*

*First published in Great Britain 1999
Silhouette Books, Eton House, 18-24 Paradise Road,
Richmond, Surrey TW9 1SR*

Special thanks and acknowledgement are given to Kristin Morgan for her contribution to the Follow That Baby mini-series

© Harlequin Book S.A. 1998

ISBN 0 373 19333 5

22-9911

*Printed and bound in Spain
by Litografia Rosés S.A., Barcelona*

KRISTIN MORGAN

lives in Lafayette, Louisiana, the very heart of Cajun country, where the French language of her ancestors is still spoken fluently by her parents and grandparents.

In addition to her writing, she enjoys cooking and preparing authentic Cajun foods for her family from recipes passed on to her through the generations. Her hobbies include reading—of course!—and gardening. She loves walking in the rain, newborn babies, all kinds of music, Christmas, chocolate desserts and love stories with happy endings. A true romantic at heart, she believes all things are possible with love.

Dear Reader,

Being a Silhouette® author means a lot to me. Silhouette has been a constant and steady support to me since they published my first novel. As a reader of romance novels, I love books about heroes and heroines who have strong emotional conflicts. As a Silhouette author, I enjoy writing stories about characters who steal my heart away in their struggle to find everlasting love.

When my agent called to say that Silhouette was inviting me to participate in a special cross-line series entitled FOLLOW THAT BABY, I was thrilled. This would be my first time to write for a special project that involved other Silhouette authors. As it turned out, it was a wonderful, fun experience.

Thanks, Silhouette, for everything.

And thanks to all my readers for your patronage.

I wish you all the romance your heart desires.

Enjoy!

Kristin Morgan

Chapter One

Sam Arquette paused momentarily to study the engraved brass nameplate on the office door. It read, Amanda Lucas, M.D. Turning the knob, he stepped inside and in one swift glance saw that the waiting room was full.

Full of pregnant women.

Well, he had been halfway expecting as much. Amanda Lucas's reputation as one of the best OB-GYN specialists in Mason's Grove, Oklahoma, was almost godlike. If he had learned anything at all about her in the past few hours, it was that she was considered the town's baby doctor extraordinaire. But the truth of the matter was, he wasn't here to see Amanda Lucas because the good folks in Mason's Grove thought the world of her. He was here as a favor to a friend.

Once again, Sam made a quick scan around the small crowded room, only to discover that he had become the center of attention. That didn't bother him. Over the years he had found there were times when his six-foot-two-inch frame made him an imposing presence to others. And as luck would have it, it seemed, this was going to be one of those times.

A moment passed. Then another. Eventually, Sam got the feeling that it was more than just his stature that had made him the center of regard. Apparently, he had stepped into a world that didn't necessarily welcome strangers—particularly, he surmised, male strangers—and for just one fleeting moment, he wished that his two young daughters were with him, although he had no earthly idea what good they would have done him, except that their being female might have somehow helped to improve his image.

And who said it was a man's world? he asked himself with a smirk.

But in spite of that wry observation, Sam felt a flush rise to his cheeks. As an ex-Navy SEABEE, he thought that he had been trained to handle any situation. But, apparently, not one where a roomful of pregnant women were scrutinizing him so warily. He felt like an alien. Like an invader of the worst kind.

Well, ex-c-u-s-e me, he thought to himself. But wasn't this a free country?

Damned right, it was.

And, frankly, he had fought more than his share of battles on foreign soil to help keep it that way. He had as much right as anyone to go anywhere he pleased.

Right?

Without a doubt.

So how, then, had he gotten himself into this...this impregnable situation, anyway?

Better yet, how could he get himself out?

Thanks a bunch, Josie, he told himself a moment later, mentally chastising his good friend, Josie Wentworth. If it hadn't been for the favor she'd asked of him, he would have been at home right this minute, doing chores around his small farm while enjoying the company of his two young children. It was his way of life these days, although sometimes the fact that it was still surprised him.

In truth, he really didn't mind doing this favor for Josie. He wanted to help the Wentworths all he could. He and Jack Wentworth, Josie's older brother, had been the best of friends. Now Jack was dead, killed only recently while on an undercover mission for the government. It seemed impossible that it could be true, but it was. And now the Wentworths were looking for a young woman whom they believed was involved with Jack right before his death. But, according to Josie, the woman had literally disappeared. Luckily, Josie had come across a doctor's statement that suggested the woman might be living in Mason's Grove. And since he now lived in the small Oklahoma town, Josie had asked him to look into the matter for her.

Clearing his throat, Sam pushed aside the sad thought that his good friend Jack was dead and, like the disciplined soldier he still was, in spite of his retirement, he focused his full attention on accomplishing his mission.

Answers. He wanted answers. For Josie and her family. For Jack. And for himself, too.

Once again, Sam cautiously surveyed the crowded waiting room. From the looks of things he figured he had made a mistake in coming to Amanda Lucas's medical office without calling for an appointment first. But these days, when it came to matters of business, he was at the mercy of his next-door neighbor, Mrs. Cunningham, who was the only person in Mason's Grove he had gotten to know well enough to have baby-sit for him. That was, when her back wasn't giving her trouble. For the most part, he spent his time being a full-time daddy to his girls. His world revolved around them. It was as simple as that.

And as complicated.

The problem was that he had been ill-prepared

to assume the responsibility of being a single parent. At the time of his wife's death, he had known more about disarming a nuclear weapon than he had about the nutritional needs of his kids. He had come a long way in the past months. Suzy Homemaker, he was not. But he was getting there.

Still, despite the fact that he was settling down to a more normal way of life than he had ever dreamed possible for himself, all within a blink of an eye of Josie Wentworth's phone call, he had felt the same old familiar stirrings of excitement that used to accompany him on every SEABEE mission he had ever gone on. Some things, it seemed, never changed. He was about as far away from that world as he could possibly get, and yet, deep down inside, he really wasn't that far away at all. Nor would he ever be, he now realized. Once a soldier, always a soldier.

Not that he was expecting this favor he was doing for the Wentworths to be any kind of a challenge. Good grief, he had just come here to ask the good lady-doctor a few questions about one of her patients. Just how difficult could that be?

Squaring his shoulders, Sam started forward, his eyes fixed on the reception area located at the rear of the waiting room. It took him five long strides to reach the counter. In the meantime, he couldn't help but notice that the decor in the room was leaning toward a very feminine influence. In fact, he was beginning to feel like a bull in a china cabinet. He was almost afraid to move, fearing he would disturb something.

Sitting behind the receptionist's desk was an attractive young brunette. She held a pen in her left hand and was jotting something down on a tablet. Settling back on his heels, Sam took a deep breath and waited for her to finish her task.

Finally, she glanced up and greeted him with a smile. "Hi. Can I help you?"

Sam grinned. It was just as he had hoped. He was going to be in and out of this place in no time at all. Simple. Uncomplicated. Not even a hint of a challenge. In some ways, that was too bad. He had been hoping for a slight adrenaline rush, at least. Oh, well, maybe next time, he told himself. "Yes, as a matter of fact, you most certainly can. I'm here to see the doctor."

"Doc Lucas?" the receptionist replied, her eyes widening somewhat. "Uh...well...yes...Doc Lucas is in," she finally stammered. "But she's with a patient right now. Is this concerning your wife?"

"My wife?" Sam repeated, his eyebrows drawing together. It took him a moment to understand what she meant. Once he did, he deepened his frown. "No—actually, I'm here on business."

"Oh, I see," she replied hesitantly. Then she cocked her head to one side. "You know, don't you, that Doc Lucas is an OB-GYN physician? All of her patients are women."

"I'm quite aware of that fact," Sam replied. "But, like I said, I'm here on business, not for medical advice. Tell me, how long will it be before I can see her?"

"Well, I don't know. That depends," the young woman said, glancing down at the appointment book in front of her. She ran her finger down a list of patients who apparently were already scheduled for that day. "Did you call earlier for an appointment, Mr....?"

Sam's grin dissolved into nothing. "No, I didn't. But, look, I'll only take a moment of her time," he said.

The receptionist began shaking her head slowly. "I'm sorry. But unless it's an emergency, Doc Lucas sees all her patients by appointment only. Perhaps you could come back on Thursday afternoon. I've just had a cancellation."

"I need to see her today," Sam argued impatiently.

"I'm sorry," the receptionist replied. "But unless you have an emergency, Dr. Lucas won't see you without an appointment. I can write your name down for three o'clock Thursday afternoon. That's the best I can offer you."

Already, Sam was shaking his head. "You don't understand," he said. "My business with Dr. Lucas is extremely important. I must see her now—today." He crossed his arms over his chest. "In fact, I'm not leaving here until I do."

After giving him a thoughtful frown, the young receptionist once again glanced down to study the list of patients she had scheduled for that day. Finally, she gazed up at him and said, "Okay, if it's that urgent, I'll see what I can do. What's your name?"

"Sam Arquette," he replied.

The young woman nodded. "Have a seat, Mr. Arquette. I'll have to speak to Doc Lucas about you." Then she turned and walked away.

Satisfied that he was finally getting somewhere—frankly, it was about time—Sam turned with the idea of taking a seat. But when he noticed that he was still the object of considerable attention—not to mention that since his arrival the delicate-looking chairs in the waiting room hadn't grown any larger to accommodate his size—Sam decided to remain standing. Once again folding his arms across his chest, he waited for the young receptionist to return.

Within a couple of minutes, she was back. "This must be your lucky day, Mr. Arquette," she announced. "Doc Lucas has agreed to see you. Follow me. I'll take you to her office."

Sam nodded and then fell right in step behind the young woman.

"Wait in here," she said when they reached the end of a corridor. "Doc Lucas is still with a patient, but she'll join you shortly."

"Thanks," he said.

"Yeah, well, maybe you shouldn't thank me just yet," the young receptionist replied.

"What do you mean?" Sam asked, a grin slipping up one side of his face.

The young woman gave him a slight smile. "Well, for one thing, Doc Lucas isn't in the best of moods today. At first, she looked aggravated when I told her about you. But then, it was as if something suddenly clicked and she changed her mind."

"What's so strange about that?"

"You don't know Doc Lucas, do you?"

Sam shook his head.

"Well, she seldom, if ever, changes her mind about anything," the receptionist said. "She runs a pretty tight ship and, for the most part, stays right on course, if you know what I mean. She's just that kind of person." With that, the young woman turned on her heel and returned to the reception area.

Sam thought he knew exactly what the receptionist meant. He had known women like that in the navy. Dr. Lucas was probably driven—focused—and totally predictable. She probably hated men and treated them like something to be conquered and then done away with. And she probably never allowed herself—or anyone else, for that matter—room for error. A regular drill sergeant. He hadn't even met her yet, but already he thought he knew her.

Alone in Amanda Lucas's office, Sam sat down to wait for his meeting with her. Minutes passed. Long, endless minutes. Finally, he picked up the only magazine he saw lying around and began reading an article on breast feeding. He figured that he might as well learn something while he waited.

Suddenly, from somewhere just behind him, he heard someone say, "Mr. Arquette, I presume."

The voice was definitely female, but it was deep and sultry and immediately sent goose bumps down his spine. There was no doubt in his mind that, under just the right circumstances, a voice like that could have easily enthralled a man—in fact, encompass his whole being. But, of course, Sam reminded himself, this wasn't the right circumstance.

Thank goodness.

Besides, even if it was, he wasn't interested. He already had his hands full, raising his two young daughters. Frankly, when the need to burn off that kind of energy hit him, he went for a long, tiring jog. And, so far, so good. It worked.

Shaking himself free of those errant thoughts, Sam sat up straight and then turned in his seat to see a woman with shoulder-length brown hair standing just a few feet inside the doorway. She had a stethoscope around her neck, and she wore a long white lab coat over her street clothes. Sam knew without a doubt that he was looking at Amanda Lucas—in fact, somehow, he had known all along that it was her voice he had heard—and in spite of himself, his heart skipped a very, very necessary beat. To add to his surprise, she didn't look at all as he had expected. She was... well...good-looking—especially for someone whom he had just recently pictured as a drill sergeant. She had clear blue eyes and a full mouth that, for the moment, at least, lacked the semblance of a smile.

But her voice... It was deep and throaty and incredibly sexy. Not just any woman deserved to have a voice like that.

Taking a deep, steadying breath, Sam stood up and quickly offered her his hand. "And you must be Dr. Lucas," he said evenly, in spite of all the weird thoughts running wild through his head. Get a grip, he told himself. He hadn't thought—nor wanted to think—of a woman in quite this way since...well, since forever, it seemed. And, truthfully, he was shaken to the core.

Amanda Lucas was shaken, too. The tall, muscular man standing before her was extremely good-looking, and for some reason that bothered her.

She folded her arms across her chest and peered down at the hand he was offering her. He had strong, capable-looking hands. Still, Amanda was contemplating whether or not to shake hands. So far her impression of Sam Arquette was that he was impulsive and arrogant. Not only that, but she was almost certain he was the same person who had been going around town earlier in the day, asking questions about her. Several of her patients had told her about him. But, finally, she resigned herself to the inevitable and slipped her hand into his, only to discover his palm was surprisingly warm for a man who was a snoop. Ending the handshake as quickly as possible, she straightened her shoulders. "My receptionist tells me that you practically insisted on seeing me this afternoon. I'm a very busy person, Mr. Arquette. I have patients waiting who need my attention. What, may I ask, is so urgent that you had to see me about it today?"

Silence followed. Clearly the man hadn't heard a word she'd uttered.

"Mr. Arquette," she said rather impatiently, once again folding her arms across her chest. She was ready to get this man out of her office. Something about him was making it difficult for her to breathe normally. Perhaps, it was because she had concluded that he was single. The look in his eyes was too aware—too aggressive—for those of a married man.

In any case, for some strange reason, her blood was pulsing through her veins at an exaggerated speed. She knew it was necessary to be firm with someone that aggressive. But every time she tried looking into his brown eyes for any length of time, she was mesmerized by their intensity. They were the color of deep, dark chocolate. "Mr. Arquette," she said again, adding a hint of frustration to her tone just to let him know she was growing impatient with him. "I'm waiting for your answer."

"Look, I need to ask you some questions about one of your patients," he finally said.

Amanda frowned. "Is that why you were snooping around town today, asking questions about me?" she demanded, her eyes never wavering from his.

"You know about that?" Sam asked, an incredulous look spreading across his face.

"Of course, I know," she replied with a smirk. "Mason's Grove is a small town, Mr. Arquette. News travels fast here."

He frowned. "What gave me away?"

Amanda almost laughed out loud on that one. Almost, but not quite. "Your looks," she replied. *Not to mention your arrogance, she thought to herself.* "Someone told me that a tall, dark-haired man was snooping around town asking questions regarding my practice, and then a couple of hours later you show up here."

"I can explain," Sam said, moving a step closer to her.

He looked menacing in a sort of nonthreatening way. If that was possible. Still, she couldn't be sure. She was determined to hold her ground.

"Good," she said, unconsciously inspecting him from head to toe and, unfortunately, finding herself enthralled with the man she saw. She chose to ignore the way something had pulled deep and hard inside of her as her eyes had traveled up and down his muscular body. "Because I feel I'm owed an explanation." Then she watched as Sam drew in a slow, deep breath.

"First off," he began, "allow me to clear up something. I'm not some weirdo, if that's what you're thinking." Amanda lifted her eyebrows in a way that suggested that was exactly what she was thinking. "And I wasn't snooping," he added gruffly—almost forcefully. "I was just trying to find out some information about you."

Amanda couldn't help herself. She wasn't about to let this man off the hook that easily. After all, he was the one who had pushed his way into her office. She was aggravated now. She wanted answers. "Then why go to my friends and neighbors? Why not come straight to me?"

"Good point," he replied evenly. "I'll remember that next time."

"Indeed," she said, giving him a hard glare. Still, her heart was beating wildly. Too wildly. She dropped her eyes from his as soon as she could. Then, drawing in a deep breath, she walked right past him to her desk. "Let me explain something to you, Mr. Arquette," she said, turning around to face him. "Any information I have concerning my patients is strictly confidential between them and me."

"I understand how you must feel about that, but—"

"When it comes to matters of this nature, Mr. Arquette, there are no buts," Amanda said, interrupting him. Frankly, she wanted to put an end to this conversation as soon as possible. She needed oxygen and there simply wasn't enough in her office right now for the two of them. "Now, if you'll excuse me, I've got a busy schedule. I'll have my receptionist show you out." With that, she headed straight past him for the door.

"Now wait a minute," he said, suddenly reaching out to stop her. In truth, he wanted to stop her for more reasons than he cared to think about. In fact, he would have liked nothing better in that moment than to chisel away her icy persona. So he had gotten off to a wrong start with the woman. Did she have to be such an iceberg about it? Where was the compassion that all doctors, male or female, were supposed to have? He was used to tangling with international spies and war criminals. Surely he could handle one small-town female doctor. Of course, the protocol in dealing with her as opposed to some war criminal was quite different. Right now, he was on his best behavior. While in the navy, not every situation required that of him.

"The least you can do is hear me out," he said meaningfully.

Immediately, her eyes dropped to where he held her arm. "Obviously, you don't understand, Mr. Arquette," Amanda said. "It's a matter of ethics. My patients trust me not to repeat our conversations." She gazed up at him, her blue eyes sparkling with indignation. "Now, if you would be so kind as to let go of my arm."

The sound of her voice swept through him like a warm, balmy breeze in springtime. Only it wasn't springtime. It was November, and the winds outside were as chilly as the glare she was giving him. Frankly, he didn't want to let her arm go. He wanted to pull her against him and kiss those pouty lips of hers. Then again, he was trying to be on his best behavior. Dammit.

"Sure thing, Doc," he said, releasing her a moment later.

Taking a deep breath, Amanda turned immediately to leave the room.

"But you're making a mistake," Sam said in her wake, in a last-ditch effort to stop her without making a scene. He was experiencing an adrenaline rush, and he knew it had to do with her somehow. With the way she had turned her back on him. He wasn't used to that kind of treatment. He was used to giving it. "It's you, Doc, who doesn't understand the seriousness of the situation. This could be a matter of life and death."

A moment passed while Amanda paused in the doorway. Finally, she spun on her heels to face him, although her expression clearly stated that she was angry at herself for giving in. She gazed at him furiously. "Okay, Mr. Arquette. You've got my undivided attention. But this had better be damned good."

Sam smirked. In spite of everything, he truly admired her spunk.

Not to mention the fact that he was in love with her voice.

He placed his hands on his hips. "Have you ever heard of the Wentworth family of Freemont Springs?" he asked.

Amanda Lucas narrowed her eyes. "Of course. Everyone in Oklahoma knows of them. Their contributions to local charities are legendary."

"So, you're aware of their reputation. Then you're also aware that they're good, honest people."

"I know that they're extremely generous with their money. But I don't know any of them personally," Amanda replied.

"Well, I do. They're close friends of mine—in fact, I'm here on their behalf. They're looking for someone. A woman by the name of Sabrina Jensen. They have reason to believe you know her. Do you?"

Of course, Amanda knew her. Sabrina Jensen was one of her OB patients. Only Sabrina had missed her last appointment and Amanda's receptionist had been unable to reach the woman to reschedule. Amanda had thought that rather odd, and had even tried to follow up on it herself, but to no avail. Now, to have this stranger asking questions about her...

"Why are the Wentworths looking for her?" Amanda asked evenly. The last thing she wanted was to give away the fact that she knew Sabrina as a patient. To her way of thinking, she saw nothing in Sam Arquette that made that information any of his business.

"Look, all I need to know is her whereabouts."

Amanda frowned. "Is she in some kind of trouble?"

"To be honest with you," Sam said, running his fingers through his hair, "the Wentworths don't know. That's why they're trying to find her."

"But I don't understand," Amanda said. "Why

are they having such a problem finding her in the first place?''

Sam frowned to himself. He wasn't accustomed to being questioned like this. As a soldier, he had been the interrogator. Now, suddenly, he found himself at the other end of the spectrum, and, frankly, it wasn't any fun. In fact, his patience with the good doctor was wearing awfully thin. "It seems," he said, "she's disappeared."

"I see. What do they think happened to her?" Amanda asked warily.

He shrugged. "That's just it. They don't know. But I can tell you this much—the Wentworths are truly concerned about her."

"Well, I'm sorry, but I can't help you with this matter."

"You can't—or you won't?" Sam replied, gazing at her intently.

Amanda had turned to leave the room, but she stopped short. She'd had about all she was going to take from this...this imposing man. Just who did he think he was? Wasn't it enough that he had her guts all tied up in knots to the point where she doubted if they would ever relax again? "Look, Mr. Arquette," she said, giving him another one of her hard glares. "Even if I knew where the woman was—which I don't—but even if I did, I wouldn't tell you."

"So, in essence," Sam began cockily, "you

would deliberately hide her whereabouts from me even if you knew them.''

Determined to keep her cool, Amanda breathed deeply. ''In essence, yes. Now, if you'll excuse me, Mr. Arquette, I have nothing more to say to you.''

Frustrated that he wasn't getting anywhere with her, Sam felt his temper flare. More than anything in that moment he wanted to shake some sense into her. For heaven's sake, couldn't she see he was only trying to help out a friend?

Sexy voice or not, Amanda Lucas had pushed him just about as far as he wanted to go. Her icy manner was becoming nothing but a pain in the behind. Frankly, it stunk. She was an iceberg, all right, through and through. He had thought he could thaw her without much effort, but he had been wrong. No doubt, one glance from her could have sunk the *Titanic*. In fact, nothing in that moment—short of kissing her senseless—would have given him greater pleasure than to have found a way to melt her down to size. His size. And then maybe she wouldn't have been so sassy.

Except for her voice. Heaven help him, but he didn't want to change a thing about her voice. It was sexy and alluring and the only thing about her that sizzled hot. In many ways, it was more than enough. He was completely and utterly enthralled with it—with the woman he suspected was hiding somewhere in that deep freeze surrounding her. But, dammit, he hated having to admit it.

"Look," he said. "The Wentworths are good people. I hope that once you think this over, you'll reconsider giving me the information they need."

"I'm sorry, Mr. Arquette, but I won't be changing my mind. Now if you'll excuse me…"

Despite Amanda's best intentions to just turn and march away, she found herself practically standing toe-to-toe with the source of her irritation. The audacity of the man. Just who did he think he was, anyway, coming into her office like this and disrupting her day? Making her feel breathless. She wasn't obligated to help him, even though he seemed to think she was.

Actually, it didn't surprise her at all that she was already at odds with him. From the moment her eyes had locked with his, she had known that he was going to be trouble. Big-time trouble. The kind of trouble she had purposely avoided for years now. Handsome. Intelligent. Cocky. He had the makings of a good old-fashioned heartbreaker. Thanks, but no thanks. Once in a lifetime was more than plenty for her. She had a purpose in life now…a reason for being. She had her patients and they needed her. And she needed them. They were her joy, her life. Perhaps, she would never totally come to terms with the way her life had turned out. Undoubtedly, she would never forget the hurt she had suffered at the hands of her ex-fiancé. But there were some things she simply had to accept.

Suddenly, Amanda realized what she was doing to herself and returned her attention to the present. "I have to get back to my patients now, Mr. Arquette. Good day."

Then she made a mental note to look into the matter of Sabrina Jensen once again. If, indeed, Sabrina was hiding out, then she was probably alone and frightened. She might even be in need of food and medical attention. But no matter the difficulties Sabrina was having to endure, Amanda would have gladly traded places with her. It had to be a wonderful feeling to be carrying the baby of the man you loved. Unfortunately, she would never know.

Once again, Amanda turned to leave the room. Just as she did, she came face-to-face with her receptionist. The young woman looked frantic. "What is it, Kathy?" Amanda asked.

"Doc Lucas," she said excitedly. "You'd better come quick. It's Lucy Foreman. She says her baby is coming—and I think she's right."

"Is she on the phone?"

"No, she's in the waiting room."

Oh, good Lord, Amanda thought. Just what she needed right now. An emergency delivery—and at her office, no less.

She hurried down the hall toward the waiting room. "Is her husband with her?"

"No," Kathy said, following alongside her. "She's alone."

"Great," Amanda muttered.

Stopping short, Amanda spun around and glared at Sam Arquette who had been following behind at a distance. "Don't leave just yet, Mr. Arquette," she said. "I may be needing your assistance. More than likely, someone is going to have to help me move my patient to an examining room."

"You're joking, right?" he replied, halting in his tracks to gape at her.

"No," Amanda said. "I'm afraid not."

Sam frowned. "I presume I have a choice in this matter."

"Of course," she answered, squaring her shoulders as if to say, if that was how he felt, she didn't really need him, after all.

But Sam figured it was costing her a lot to ask him for his help. If there was one thing he had already come to realize about Dr. Amanda Lucas, she wasn't a woman who liked having to depend on a man for anything. Well, hey, that wasn't his problem.

"Okay, Doc," he said. "I'm in."

In a heartbeat, Amanda turned and rushed down the hallway toward her patient.

As Sam followed at her heels, he couldn't help but wonder what he was getting himself into.

Chapter Two

Now that Amanda had a moment to think over what she had just done, she had no idea what had made her decide to get *him* involved. Stupidity, she supposed. Initially, she had thought that, under the circumstances, Sam could have come in handy. But even if that did turn out to be the case, it didn't excuse the fact that he was arrogant and demanding, and that any woman with a lick of sense could have easily seen that about him, first and foremost, before noticing how handy he might have been. But was she looking at him with a lick of sense?

Uh-uh. Oh, no, not her. From the moment she had laid eyes on him, she had yet to use an ounce of her brain power.

Which told her one thing. She had better get a

grip on herself—and quick. She didn't have time to be toying around with thoughts of Sam Arquette. At this very moment, she had an emergency on her hands.

Still, Amanda found that her heart was pounding like crazy at the idea that Sam Arquette was following close on her heels and that if she so much as paused, even for a second, he would be right on top of her.

Needless to say, she didn't pause, not even as she swung open the door leading from the back part of her office into the waiting room area. The last thing she wanted was to have Sam Arquette on top of her. In fact, the very thought of it left her feeling breathless.

"Has anyone called an ambulance?" she asked, taking in some badly needed air. She had several reasons for needing it. Of course, the number one reason was Sam Arquette himself. The man was...well...suffocating.

"No, not yet," Kathy replied.

"Then do it," Amanda ordered, hurrying forward.

Within a split second of scanning the entire waiting room, Amanda saw Lucy Foreman hunched over in a chair in one corner of the room. Crouched down at Lucy's feet was Sheré, Amanda's nurse. She was taking Lucy's blood pressure.

Amanda hurried over, then bent down in front of her patient. "What's going on, Lucy?" she asked, trying to evaluate the situation for herself. For the moment, at least, Sam Arquette was nowhere within her immediate thoughts. Still, her pulse was racing from the urgency of the moment—and, regardless of what else she told herself, from the fact that it was him, she knew, who was now standing right behind her, practically breathing down her neck. As a result, chills ran rabid down her spine.

But, regardless of her reaction to Sam Arquette, one thing was becoming perfectly clear to her.

Ready or not, there was a baby on the way, and it looked as though he or she wasn't planning to wait around very much longer for the rest of the world to figure that out.

"It's the baby, Dr. Lucas," Lucy cried out.

"I know, Lucy," Amanda said in a comforting voice. "But don't worry. Everything is going to be okay. Where's Tom?"

Tom was not only Lucy's husband, but he was also supposed to be her coach during labor.

"At a cattle auction in Freemont Springs," Lucy replied, tears brimming in her eyes.

Amanda stood and drew in a deep breath. Freemont Springs was almost two hours away from Mason's Grove. There was no way Tom Foreman could make it back to Mason's Grove in time to be at his wife's bedside for the birth of their first child. One thing about babies, they were notorious for ignoring the readiness of others and coming into this old world when they were good and ready.

And, without a doubt, Lucy's baby was ready.

"I can't do this without Tom," Lucy cried out.

"Of course, you can," Amanda said, giving her patient a warm, reassuring smile. In her experience as an OB doctor, it never failed that when a woman went into labor, the one person she wanted at her side was the man she loved. But sometimes that simply wasn't possible. She thought of Sabrina Jensen. If Mr. Arquette's story was true, the young waitress would have to deliver her baby into the world all alone. As a woman, Amanda allowed herself a moment to feel sad for Sabrina; however, as a physician, she knew she had to get a grip and focus on what was happening right now.

"I know you were counting on Tom being here with you," she said, gazing at Lucy, "but it doesn't look like that's going to happen. Just think about it, honey," she added, her whole manner growing serious, but confident. "You could do this all by yourself if you had to. But, of course, you don't have to. I'll be with you every step of the way."

After a moment's pause, Amanda's words seemed to sink in, and Lucy nodded in agreement.

Assured in her ability to get her patient through

her labor without the added guidance of a labor coach, Amanda moved quickly to get her office ready for the unexpected delivery. Still, she took a moment to give Lucy a reassuring hug.

Turning with the idea of giving her staff additional instructions on what to do next, Amanda was startled to find herself face-to-face with Sam Arquette.

Well, they weren't exactly face-to-face. It was more like face-to-chest. Her face. His chest. Her eye level was just below the base of his throat— in fact, right above the V opening of his sport shirt. Never in her life had she been so starkly aware of the dark, springy hair that grew on a man's chest. Not even in med school. He swallowed, and without much upward movement of her eyes, Amanda watched his Adam's apple bob up and down. Her breath lodged in her throat. The whole thing gave her the silliest feeling in the pit of her stomach. Then she lifted her eyes a few inches higher, and *wham!* They locked with his.

He grinned knowingly, as though somehow he knew about the silly feeling in the pit of her stomach and the breathlessness that was presently making her feel almost light-headed. "What do you want me to do?" he asked.

For some reason, that question was enough to suck out any air that was left in her lungs. If she ever decided to allow herself a naughty moment, there would have been plenty of things she would have liked to have seen him do. But, of course, she never allowed herself such things.

"Uh…" she stammered, mentally shaking herself free of the unconscious hold he had on her. "I need to get Lucy Foreman to one of the examining rooms in the back. Can you help me?"

A cocky, lopsided grin slid up one side of Sam's face. "I can do better than that," he said, brushing past her and lifting Lucy into his arms. "I can get her there myself."

In his sudden move to get to her patient, he had rubbed his arm across Amanda's breasts. Without actually looking at her, he mumbled an apology.

"Uh—no problem," Amanda answered.

But, of course, there was a problem.

A big problem.

Her nipples were squeezed tight. And the tingling sensation in the pit of her stomach persisted.

Amanda was rattled, no doubt about it. Still, she refused to accept what was happening to her. She had come too far from her past experience with men to allow some arrogant so-and-so to walk into her world and shake it up.

Taking a deep, steadying breath, Amanda straightened her shoulders. "Have you ever done this before, Mr. Arquette?" she asked, adding a slight edge to her voice. It was intentional, of course. She wanted to make sure that the distance she planned to keep from him was well-defined. She only hoped he had gotten her message.

Sam gave her the most incredulous-looking smile. "What—carry a woman?"

Amanda felt a blush rise to her cheeks. She had no idea why she had asked him such a dumb question. Of course, a guy like him had carried a woman before. Plenty of times, no doubt. And straight up to bed, she was more than willing to bet. Nonetheless, determined now to see this moment through, she met his stare evenly. "I was referring to the fact that Lucy's in labor," she added for clarification.

The corners of Sam's mouth twitched up. "Well, now that you mention it, I once came to the rescue of a pregnant woman." He tightened his hold on Lucy. "But it's a long story. We probably don't have time for it right now."

Lucy groaned.

Amanda felt another wave of heat rise to her face.

"N-no, of course not," she finally stammered after coming to her senses. Still, she found herself intensely curious about his story—particularly about the pregnant woman. And though she usually minded her own business, she would have liked nothing better in that moment than to have heard its details. "Follow me," she commanded instead.

"I want Tom with me," Lucy wailed, wrapping her arms around Sam's neck.

They reached the nearest examining room. "Place her in here," Amanda said. Sam entered the room and gently laid Lucy down on the examining table that had been made ready for her just moments ago. Then he stepped back, clearly with the intention of leaving the room.

Reaching out, Lucy grabbed hold of his arm. "Don't leave me," she cried. "Please…"

Startled, Sam gaped at her. Finally, he said, "I'm not what you need, Lucy. I'm not a doctor."

"I don't care," she cried out. "Tom's not here. Please don't leave me."

Sam glanced up, his startled gaze meeting Amanda's. His eyes probed hers and he didn't blink once during the following few seconds. But finally, unable to deal with the intensity of the moment, Amanda had to look away. Shrugging her shoulders, she said, "If Lucy wants you to stay, that's fine with me."

Looking completely bewildered, Sam shook his head from side to side. "Now wait a minute," he said, his hands perched on his hips. "You've got the wrong guy here. That story I mentioned a moment ago had nothing whatsoever to do with delivering any baby. The woman just happened to be pregnant. Period. I don't know the first thing about women having babies."

Which was the truth, Sam realized. On both occasions when his girls had been born, he had been out of the country on a mission.

"It's not all that difficult," Amanda found herself saying. "All you have to do is tell her when to breathe and when to push."

Once again, Sam's eyes met Amanda's. And, once again, the encounter did strange things to her. Things she would have preferred not to have to recognize. Suddenly, she felt hot all over.

"Is that all there is to it?" he asked.

"That's it," she replied breathlessly—and she was completely aggravated with herself for feeling that way.

But, in spite of everything, Amanda had a feeling that Sam Arquette was quite capable of filling in as Lucy's labor coach. In fact, she had a feeling that he was quite capable of doing anything he put his mind to.

"Well, Mr. Arquette, you're going to have to hurry and make up your mind on this one," Amanda stated in no uncertain terms. "As you can see, there isn't much time. Either you're in or out. So what's it going to be?"

It was going to have to be out, Sam told himself. This was one time he was in way over his head.

He sucked in a deep breath and tried to find the right words to explain his decision to the lady-doctor and her patient. Surely once he did, they would understand why he couldn't be a part of this.

But then Lucy started moaning, again.

And then Sam remembered something.

Something very vital to his nature.

There was no way he could ever live with himself if he turned his back on a woman in need.

He simply wasn't made that way.

Regardless of the circumstances.

Dammit.

He slipped off his bomber jacket and threw it in a far corner of the room. Then he began rolling up the sleeves of his shirt. "Okay, tell me what I have to do," he said, resigning himself to the inevitable.

Amanda was impressed, both with the man and his decision to stick by Lucy when it was obvious that wasn't what he really wanted to do. "Stand at her head," she instructed him. He quickly moved into that position. "Now," she added, "when I give the word, lift her shoulders slightly off the table and instruct her to push hard. When she isn't pushing, you want her breathing like this." She demonstrated the technique. "Got it?"

"Got it," he replied.

But it wasn't long before Sam realized that he didn't have it quite like he thought. Giving birth was a laborious job.

In fact, it was downright exhausting, and he was only the coach. Lucy had to do all the work. Poor woman. If she wasn't pushing so hard that her face was turning as red as a beet, she was working hard at breathing correctly. Amanda Lucas was the coolest person there. She was in total control. Thank goodness, someone was, he thought.

But Amanda was anything but cool. As a doctor, she was in control of the situation. But as a woman, practically forced into the company of a man she found extremely attractive, she was on fire. Burning up. Nonetheless, this was her moment of glory—her reason for deciding to specialize in prenatal care and delivery. If she couldn't have children of her own, she would help other women give birth. Somehow, even if it was vicariously, it helped to ease the ache inside of her. Right now was a moment of joy...a moment of complete wonderment.

Amanda's heart began to pound. "It won't be long now, Lucy," she said. "The baby's crowning." Then, without actually glancing up at Sam, she added, "Are you all right?"

"Uh—yeah—sure," Sam replied. "Is the baby coming?"

"Uh-huh...a couple more minutes should do it," Amanda said.

"That's it?" he asked in awe.

Amanda gazed up at him momentarily. "You're doing fine, Mr. Arquette. Hang in there just a few minutes longer. A good way to stay focused is to think of this baby as your child being born.''

''Is it a boy?'' he said, grinning. ''I always wanted a boy.''

For some silly reason, Amanda's heart sank to the floor. ''Then this should be easy for you.''

''Not as easy as it looks for you.''

''I've done this many times, Mr. Arquette,'' she reminded him.

At that moment, Lucy gave a loud moan.

Amanda drew in a deep breath. ''Come on, Lucy,'' she said, turning her total concentration back to her patient. ''Give me one more big, hard push, and I promise your baby will be born. Come on, you can do it.''

''Yeah, Lucy, you can do it,'' Sam added enthusiastically.

A moment later, with a smile of pure contentment on her face, Amanda assisted as the baby slipped from Lucy's body and into Amanda's caring hands. Seconds later, the newborn was crying on his own. ''He's beautiful, Lucy,'' Amanda said.

''I wish Tom were here,'' Lucy replied in a voice filled with tearful joy.

From the doorway someone announced that the ambulance had just arrived.

The baby was really squalling now. Amanda finished with what she had to do for her patient and then gave the newborn to her nurse who wrapped him in a blanket. Soon the crying infant was in his mother's arms.

Lucy was crying and laughing while cuddling her baby against her. Sam found himself choked up with emotion, as well. Experiencing a birth firsthand was…well, powerful stuff, even for an ex-soldier who thought he had seen it all.

His eyes met Amanda's, and she gave him a joyous smile unlike any she had given him thus far. And yet, for just a moment, Sam sensed something very sad in it. He couldn't quite put his finger on what it was, but it was there, hidden just beneath the curve of her lips. In more ways than he cared to think about, Amanda Lucas intrigued him.

And, heaven help him, Sam thought, but he had always been a sucker for a good, challenging puzzle.

Amanda's staff and the ambulance personnel worked together to prepare Lucy and her baby for their trip to the hospital. Lucy thanked Sam again and again, and even said that she and her husband were going to invite him over to their ranch for dinner one night soon. She made Sam promise that he would come.

"I could use a cup of coffee. How about you?" Amanda asked as soon as Lucy and her baby were in the ambulance and on their way, all safe and sound.

"That sounds like a winner," Sam replied.

She motioned toward a closed door. "You can clean up in there," she said.

A few minutes later, after rejoining Sam in the hallway, she led him to the coffee room where a fresh pot was done brewing. She had the greatest staff in the world. "Thanks, Kathy," she said, loud enough for her receptionist to hear.

"You're welcome," Kathy replied.

Amanda poured two cups of coffee. "Sugar? Cream?" she asked.

"Black," he replied.

After giving him his cup and leaning one hip against the counter, Amanda blew on the surface of her coffee. Then, glancing up, she said, "Since it seems I have a moment, I'd like to hear about that story you mentioned earlier."

Sam frowned. "What story?"

"The one where you rescued a pregnant woman."

"Oh, that story," Sam replied.

"Uh-huh," Amanda said, taking a sip of her coffee. She pretended that her inquiry was simple curiosity—and, in fact, that was all it was, she tried to tell herself.

Sam shrugged. "It really isn't much of a story. I was in Bosnia some years ago on a mission for the navy. As it turned out, I ran across this woman who had gotten caught in the cross fire of a battle going on near her home. Like I said, she was preg-

nant. Anyway, I got her to safety. That's all there
was to it.''

"So, you're a war hero," she said evenly.

"I can assure you, I'm no hero. I was just doing
my job.''

Amanda's heart picked up tempo. She wasn't all
that sure she could agree with him on that one.
Lucy Foreman certainly thought he was a hero. In
any case, Amanda wasn't about to argue the point
with him. "Are you still in the navy?" she asked.

"No. I retired a year ago. Personal reasons," he
said. For a moment, Sam thought about spilling his
guts to her, but he decided not to. The busy doctor
probably didn't have time for his problems, anyway. Nor did she want to hear them. "Look," he
said, sighing deeply, "I don't suppose you've
changed your mind about giving me the information I asked for earlier.''

Amanda immediately stiffened. "No, I haven't
changed my mind.''

Sam placed his empty coffee cup in the sink. "I
didn't think you had," he replied, giving her a
thorough once-over that sent electric jolts down her
body.

Amanda knew he was trying to intimidate her—
and, frankly, it was working. Her confidence in
herself as a doctor was infallible and not even the
sexiest grin on his face right now could change
that. But for years her confidence in herself as a

woman had often stood on shaky ground, and just about any good, strong shakedown—like the one Sam Arquette was presently giving her—was enough to send her emotions into a tailspin. Which was ridiculous of her, she knew. This was the twentieth century, for heaven's sake. Just because she was infertile didn't make her any less of a woman.

Right?

Right.

As though Sam sensed it was time for him to make his exit, he shoved himself away from the cabinet and headed for the door. "Well, see you around, Doc," he said offhandedly.

Amanda released a deep breath. Hadn't she been counting the seconds until he would leave her office? Why then, she wondered, did she suddenly feel so...so let down. "I doubt it," she replied stiffly. "I stay busy and don't get out much."

He gave a small laugh. "Ouch," he said, grinning at her. "Is that your way of telling me to get lost? Because if it is, let me assure you, you've got my intentions all wrong. I was just being polite."

Amanda felt her face flush. "Well, let me assure you, if that's what you think, you've got me all wrong. I'm a busy person. I don't have time for any of this. Thank you for assisting me, Mr. Arquette," she continued, now in a very formal tone of voice. "But I must get back to my patients.

Good day.'' She strolled past him and disappeared down the hall.

Sam stood there and watched her go. In spite of himself, he had to smile. Amanda Lucas was one of the most stubborn women he had ever met. She had spunk. And a temper that flared hot at a moment's notice. Still, she touched something in him. A nerve, perhaps. Nonetheless, it had left an impression on him that he knew he wasn't likely to forget any time soon.

It was late that evening when Amanda finally finished making her rounds at the hospital. And what a stressful day she'd had, she thought as she climbed into her car and headed for home. All she could think about doing was getting under the spray of her shower and staying there until all the hot water in the tank ran out. This was one day, by golly, she had earned it.

In fact, she wished that she could simply tune out the world for a while—especially her thoughts of Sam Arquette. They were driving her crazy. Not only that, but since his visit to her office, she was even more concerned about Sabrina Jensen. Actually, she knew very little about Sabrina, other than the fact that the young waitress was pregnant and had been in her care for several months when she failed to show up for her monthly checkup. Amanda's receptionist had tried calling her right away to reschedule, only to discover that the telephone number Sabrina had given them was bogus, and her mailing address failed to yield her whereabouts. Amanda hadn't heard from the young woman since. But now, more than ever, she wished that she knew where her patient was, if for no other reason than to verify that she was all right.

Damn Sam Arquette anyway, for showing up in her life. He was the most arrogant, infuriating, stubborn, willful man she knew. Just as she'd thought, he was turning out to be nothing but trouble.

Suddenly, without any warning whatsoever, the engine of her car died. Just like that, everything—headlights, radio, power steering and brakes—went dead, leaving her stunned as to what was happening. Somehow, she managed to maneuver the car to the shoulder of the road where she tried the ignition. Nothing happened. She waited a moment and then tried again. Once more, the engine failed to start. She tried again and again, but the result was always the same.

Sitting back in her seat, Amanda gave a deep, frustrated sigh. She knew absolutely nothing about cars. They either started, or they didn't.

In her case, it didn't.

Now what? she thought.

Dropping her hands into her lap, Amanda told herself to stay calm. Perhaps, the next time she tried the ignition, the car would crank without mishap.

A few seconds later, she tried again, but still the engine stalled.

Okay, she told herself with a deep sigh. Should she just stay put and use her cellular phone to call for help? Or should she get out and walk to the nearby house? After all, she knew the older couple who lived there. She had gone to school with their son.

Before she could make up her mind, Amanda saw headlights approaching in her rearview mirror and realized that help was already on its way. One thing about living in a town the size of Mason's Grove, there was an outstandingly good chance that she would know the person driving that vehicle. It might even be one of her neighbors. She put her emergency lights on and waited for the car to reach her. Since the temperature outside had been dropping rapidly since nightfall, Amanda turned up the collar of her coat. In spite of her calm exterior, her heart was racing at an accelerated speed.

Finally, the vehicle slowed, practically coming to a stop alongside her. Amanda didn't recognize the black pickup. Suddenly, the possibility that the person inside the cab could be a complete stranger sent chills down her spine. Growing even more apprehensive, she checked to make sure that the doors of her car were locked and then reached for her cellular telephone to call for help.

The driver of the truck pulled to the shoulder of the road right in front of her car. A second later, just as she was beginning to dial an emergency operator on her cellular phone, a man opened the driver's side door and stepped to the ground. There was something very familiar about him and Amanda's heart slammed against her chest. He began walking toward her car, and even in the darkness, she saw that his black bomber jacket stretched across his shoulders. Oh-oh, she thought, feeling a weakening in the pit of her stomach. It looked as though trouble had indeed arrived on the scene.

He strolled right up to her window with a broad grin on his handsome face and the weakness in Amanda's stomach oozed all the way down to her knees. "Hi," he said. "Looks like we meet again. I bet you never expected it to be so soon."

Amanda smiled back. She couldn't help herself. It was as if his grin were contagious. Besides, what choice did she have other than to go along with him? No matter how she felt about him, right this very moment Sam Arquette was her angel of mercy.

Then, within a fraction of a second, Amanda had a more sinister thought about him, and her face lost all expression. "Did you do this?" she asked, her eyes narrowing.

His eyebrows pulled together. "Do what?" he replied.

"Do this," Amanda gestured, certain now that what she thought about him was true. From the way he had practically forced himself into her office earlier today, she wouldn't put it past him to do whatever he thought necessary to get what he wanted from her. Or to get even. Well, she had news for him. This female wasn't about to fold under pressure. Swinging open her car door, Amanda got out and placed her hands on her hips. "Did you do this to get even with me?"

Sam gaped at her. "Just what are you suggesting?" he asked, placing his hands on his hips. They were staring each other down, and, so far, neither of them had blinked.

"I'm suggesting that you sabotaged my car, so that you could come along like this and pretend to be the Good Samaritan."

"Would you mind giving me your logic in that?"

"It's quite simple," she said smugly. "You thought I'd be so grateful to you that I'd give in and tell you everything you want to know about Sabrina Jensen."

"Is that a fact?" he said, grinning at her.

"It is," she replied haughtily.

"So…" he said, still grinning at her. "You're finally admitting that Sabrina Jensen is a patient of yours."

"I didn't say that."

"Well, you damned sure implied it."

"You're taking what I said all out of context."

"Am I?"

"Yes. You're the one who thinks I have information on her. But I didn't once say that I did."

Frowning at her, Sam spread his feet apart as though he were getting ready for a good fight. As though he had been wrongly accused and was bound and determined to correct the injustice. Amanda's stomach bottomed out and it was her first indication that maybe she had misjudged his motive in stopping to help her.

If so, she was quite certain that it was the only thing about him so far that she had misjudged.

Narrowing his eyes, Sam said, "You're crazy, Doc, if you think I'd sabotage your car. Believe me, I know easier and quicker ways of getting a person to tell me what I want to know."

Amanda wasn't sure if she was supposed to take that as a threat or not. In any case, she believed he probably knew plenty of ways to make a woman talk—in or out of bed. The thought of him trying to make her talk had her pulse points throbbing out of control. Determined to hold her ground,

Amanda crisscrossed her arms and glared back at him.

"Look," he finally said in a gentler voice. "It's your choice to believe me or not. But I didn't do anything to your car."

Taking a deep breath, Amanda dropped her arms to her sides and glanced off in the distance. For some strange reason, she believed him. She truly did. He was capable of anything, she knew. Still, there was a strong code of ethics about him. He played by the rules—even if they were his rules. "Okay, I believe you," she remarked offhandedly. "I'm sorry I jumped to the wrong conclusion."

Sam Arquette gave her a genuine grin. "Well, it seems the good doctor is humble, after all. In that case, apology accepted."

"Thank you," she replied. In spite of his good humor, something about him told Amanda that under no circumstances should she allow this man to get the better of her.

"I'm not a mechanic," he said, "but I do know about cars. I can take a look under your hood if you want me to."

Amanda shook her head. "No, that's all right. It's getting late. I'll just call a towing service and have it brought to a mechanic."

She had just turned to get her cellular phone from the front seat of her car when, from out of nowhere, she heard the sweetest little voice say, "Daddy, can we go home now?"

Whirling around in surprise, Amanda saw a young child hanging out the driver's window of Sam's truck. She had long, dark ringlets of hair that fell to her shoulders. The resemblance between the child and Sam was so striking, Amanda was stunned speechless.

"In a minute, sweetheart," Sam replied. "I'm trying to help the lady. She has car trouble. Now sit back down in the seat and stay quiet like I told you and Caroline to do."

"Oh, okay," the child said, and then her face disappeared from view.

Amanda gaped at Sam. Finding her voice, she asked, "Who's she?"

"Sara," he replied evenly. "My youngest daughter."

"You have children?" she asked, a strange, quivering feeling settling in the pit of her stomach. Oh, for heaven's sake, he had children. He, of all people.

"Yeah," he said, grinning widely. "I have two girls. One is six and the other is nearly four."

By now Amanda's heart was in her throat. "I guess I should have realized that you were married, but for some reason—your manner this afternoon in my office, I suppose—I didn't think you were."

She glanced down at his hands. "You aren't wearing a wedding band."

While there was something about him that said he was off-limits, Amanda still couldn't believe that it was because he was a married man with kids. He didn't seem to be the kind of guy to give his heart to any woman. Obviously, she was wrong.

"My wife died suddenly just over a year ago."

"Oh—I'm sorry," she said.

"Yeah," he said, glancing thoughtfully toward his truck. "It's been especially tough on the girls."

Amanda gazed toward his truck. It was indeed tragic that his children's mother had to die so young. Little girls needed their mothers. She knew that better than most. Her own mother had died when she was four. And if Sam was anything like her father, he had no idea what to do with his children. And that, she knew firsthand, could be the most tragic thing of all.

He turned his gaze back to Amanda. "I guess you've had a pretty rough day, huh?"

Amanda smiled. "Sort of." And then she heard Sam's daughter's sweet little voice again.

"Daddy..." the child said hesitantly.

At the sound of his name, Sam turned once again in the direction of the truck. Amanda looked that way, too.

Sara was back, leaning out the window. Only

this time she had a pained look on her face. "I need to go, Daddy—bad."

"Okay, Sara," Sam replied. Glancing at Amanda, he said, "Look, I'm going to have to get her home. Why don't you ride along with us, and once Sara is done we'll take you back to your place?"

"Why don't we just take her straight to my house?" Amanda said, surprising herself for suggesting such a thing. She never invited company to her house. But it was too late now to recall her words. "I live less than a mile up the road. We'll be there in no time."

Sam frowned. "But that's a lot of trouble for you."

"It's the least I can do. You would be home by now if you hadn't stopped to help me."

"But are you sure you don't mind?"

"No, I don't mind."

And the truth was, now that she gave it some thought, she really didn't.

And that, she supposed, was what bothered her the most about this whole scene.

In fact, it bothered her a lot.

It was as though she were playing the part of some other woman.

But then, there was more here to be considered than just her feelings. Sitting inside the cab of that truck were two little girls who had lost their mother.

Amanda couldn't help herself. Her heart went straight out to them.

Chapter Three

Amanda walked to the passenger side of Sam's truck and opened the door. Sam got in on his side. For just a moment his two little girls gazed at Amanda with wide, speculative eyes and then quickly scooted over to their father's side, giving her plenty of room to climb aboard.

"Dr. Amanda Lucas, these are my two daughters, Caroline and Sara," Sam said.

"Hello, there," Amanda said, smiling at them.

"Hi," they replied together. Then they glanced curiously at their father.

Sam cranked the engine of his truck. "Dr. Lucas's car won't start, so we're going to take her home."

"But I gotta go, Daddy," Sara replied in a somewhat panicky voice.

"Don't worry, Sara," Sam replied. "Dr. Lucas said you can use her bathroom, okay?"

Once again, the child turned and observed Amanda, this time with a critical eye. Finally, she said, "Do you give shots?"

Ah, Amanda thought, so that was it. The word *doctor* had spooked her. "Well, yes, Sara," she answered carefully, hoping to calm the child's fears. "Sometimes I don't have any other choice. Sometimes an injection is the best way for me to treat my patients."

"Oh," Sara replied in a lowered voice, obviously disappointed in Amanda's answer. Then the child turned her head to look at her father. "Am I going to get a shot, Daddy?" she asked, her small voice filled with uncertainty.

"Of course not, Sara," Sam answered. "You're not sick, are you?"

The child shook her head. "Uh-uh."

"So there's nothing to be worried about. Dr. Lucas and I are just friends." He looked over at Amanda and winked as if to say he knew he was stretching the truth somewhat, but for her to please go along with him for now.

And, of course, she would, for the little girls' sakes.

While Sam followed her directions to her house, she found herself unconsciously staring at him. Suddenly, he glanced at her and she was caught in the act. Blushing a deep red, she quickly turned her head in the opposite direction. Funny thing was, in some strange way, she had been admiring him. He might have been an impatient man in her office today, but with his children he seemed to have all the patience in the world. He loved them dearly, she could tell. Sara and Caroline were lucky. Amanda had never had that kind of protection in her life. Her father had allowed her to raise herself after her mother's death. And her ex-fiancé—well, when it turned out she wasn't perfect, his so-called love had cooled down to a deep freeze in no time at all.

But she was willing to bet that Sam Arquette wasn't like that. Even though she hardly knew him, he seemed the kind of man who had a backbone of steel. He would be there for those he loved through thick and thin. It was that strength of conviction that she was finding totally irresistible.

And, according to her way of thinking, that meant trouble. Because no matter how dependable someone appeared to be, there was always that chance that she was being fooled.

So why then, with all of her clearheaded thinking, was her heart still beating so fast?

And why did she feel this bond between them?

Surprisingly, her answer had to do with kids. First, there was Lucy's baby, and now his own children. Correction. His *motherless* children. She reached out and gently stroked Caroline's hair, and then Sara's. Both of them turned and smiled at her. She smiled back.

Then Caroline sat up straight in her seat and with the innocence of a child said, "Mrs. Cunningham is going to be awfully glad to hear you have a girlfriend, Daddy. She says you need one."

At the mention of his next-door neighbor and trusted baby-sitter, Sam gave a small laugh. "I see Mrs. Cunningham has been at it again. One of these days Mrs. Cunningham is going to have to learn to mind her own business."

"Azalea Cunningham?" Amanda asked.

"Uh—yeah," Sam replied, giving her a quick glance. "You know her?"

"Of course. I know practically everyone in town," she replied smugly.

Sam basked in the sound of her voice. It was so deep and throaty. In spite of her coldness toward him, it made him think of warm, sultry nights and red-hot sex. His blood was beginning to boil at the mere thought of the two of them together. Man, was he ever losing control.

Immediately pushing those dangerous thoughts aside, he cleared his throat. "I bought the farm next door to Mrs. Cunningham about a year ago and she baby-sits the girls for me sometimes. The kids love her." He shrugged. "I think she's great, too."

Amanda glanced his way. "It's just that you would like her to mind her own business."

"Exactly," he said. "I don't know why, but for some reason, she has the idea that she needs to mother me like she does my girls."

"And you don't agree with her?"

"Well..." he said, suddenly grinning from ear to ear. "Maybe just a little."

That grin of his was enough to send Amanda's resolve spiraling to the floor. And, in spite of the fact that she suddenly felt flushed, goose bumps shimmied down her spine.

She was losing it, all right. Big time.

He was, she quickly decided, too good-looking for his own good.

She looked away. What was wrong with her? Didn't she have the strength to resist a simple little smile? She couldn't believe that after all these years of disciplining herself, she would weaken this easily. This quickly. Suddenly realizing that they were nearing her street, she said, "Take the next right."

"I was planning to," he replied with that same boyish grin on his face.

Of course, he knew exactly where she lived, Amanda realized with a smirk. She suspected he hadn't even needed her general directions. He'd probably asked someone in town. Still irritated with him for snooping into her business, she gazed out the passenger's side window.

Moments later, Sam pulled into Amanda's driveway. "We're here," he said.

"I'm cold, Daddy," Caroline said.

Amanda glanced down at Sara and Caroline, and saw that Sara was squirming in her seat. "I still gotta go, Daddy," the child said. Opening the passenger door, Amanda jumped to the ground, then rushed toward her front door to unlock it. She had it wide open by the time Sam, Caroline and Sara reached her. Flicking on several light switches, she said, "The bathroom is down the hall to your left."

"Caroline, stay here with Amanda," Sam instructed, quickly taking Sara by the hand and leading her down the hall. "We'll be right back."

"I'm thirsty, Daddy," Caroline said.

Amanda smiled. "We'll be in the kitchen getting her some water," Amanda replied, slipping her hand into Caroline's and leading her toward the kitchen.

The child followed so trustingly that it touched something deep within Amanda. Something that was vulnerable and raw, even after all these years of knowing she could never have children of her own. At one point she had entertained thoughts of adopting. But by then, her career was in full swing and she had convinced herself it would be enough in the long run to make her happy. And for her own good, she had never allowed herself to examine that decision too closely. Until now. Until she felt the warmth of Caroline's small hand tucked in hers. Now she wondered if she had made the right decision.

A couple of minutes later Sara came rushing into the kitchen ahead of her father.

Suddenly, Amanda got the crazy idea to make hot cocoa for the girls—and, of course, for their father, too. Crazy, because it wasn't something she would normally do. Other than a few charitable functions, she kept pretty much to herself. She didn't feel the need to be social. Her career kept her too busy for that. Oh, sure, she did get lonely at times. Nothing, not even professional success, came without a price. But tonight, she wanted to make an exception. Tonight, she felt like having company for a while. She was enjoying Sam's children so much. And, as much as she hated to admit it, a part of herself that she'd thought long dead came alive when Sam was near.

"Caroline. Sara. How would you like a cup of cocoa before going home?"

Widening their eyes, Caroline and Sara glanced at their father who was now standing in the doorway. "Can we, Daddy?" Sara asked.

"Please, Daddy?" Caroline pleaded half a second later.

Glancing his way, Amanda held her breath and waited for his answer.

"No, not tonight, girls," Sam replied, shaking his head. Then, after rubbing the back of his neck, he glanced at Amanda and added, "It's getting past their bedtime."

"Oh, please, Daddy," his girls said in unison.

"We never go anywhere," Caroline added.

"It's instant cocoa. It won't take but a minute," Amanda chimed in on their behalf.

Finally, after gazing at Amanda in a way that suggested he could have strangled her bare-handed for extending such an offer in the first place, Sam said, "Oh, all right. But we'll have to make it quick." Turning his complete attention to Amanda, he added, "Look, are you sure about this? My girls are great, but sometimes—especially when they're tired—they can be quite a handful."

Amanda bent down between his daughters, placed her arms around their waists and hugged them against her. Sara leaned her small head against Amanda's. The little girls seemed open to her affection and that was all that mattered to her for now. "I'm sure," she said. She hugged his girls one more time and then stood to prepare the cocoa.

By now, Sam was leaning one shoulder against the door frame, his arms crossed over his chest. He watched, at first in amusement, as his young daughters attempted to help Amanda prepare the cocoa, and he was amazed by the camaraderie already existing among the three of them. A camaraderie he wasn't sure he liked. He didn't know what Amanda Lucas's game was, but if it included more than a friendly cup of cocoa, he wasn't interested. His kids were his world, and the last thing he wanted for them was a stepmother like the self-centered, uncaring one he and his brother had had. It hadn't taken them long to learn that when in her presence, they were to behave like well-disciplined children. In other words, seen but never heard. His girls had already been through enough in the past year, losing their mother and then having to put up with a full-time dad who was doing his best to fill the void left by her death. They didn't need a stepmother. To his way of thinking, the odds were too great that Amanda would only add to their problems. Thanks, but no thanks. He was all his girls would ever need. And they were all he was ever going to need. End of story.

Besides, being a full-time father didn't exactly give him much time for any kind of social life. He was so focused on raising his two girls that he hadn't touched a woman—let alone thought about sex—in such a long time he'd almost forgotten what it was like.

Almost.

But not quite.

The problem was, for some cockamamy reason, being around Amanda was making him remember.

Not that she seemed to have much of a social life. From what he'd seen so far of her house, it was barren of anything resembling a relationship with family, or even close friends. If there was one thing the good folks of Mason's Grove had consistently said about their baby doctor's personal life, it was that she was a loner. And from what he'd seen of her so far, he was inclined to believe them.

Pushing himself away from the door frame, he strolled to where Amanda stood at the counter with her back to him. "Almost done?" he said, stopping right behind her.

"Almost," she replied, obviously startled by his nearness.

"Smells good," he said, deliberately leaning over her shoulder in order to see what she was doing. He also liked smelling her perfume. "Is there anything I can do to help? I don't want the girls and me to be a burden."

By now, Amanda's insides were going nuts. Sam's face was right next to hers. She hadn't been this close to a man in…well…years. It was intoxicating. Her knees were as weak as a newborn calf's.

Suddenly, Sam placed his hand at the small of her back.

And that was her undoing. A pressure began to build in her, and at any given moment she felt certain she was going to explode.

Lucky for Amanda, she didn't explode. Instead, she suffered a meltdown. But no matter how she looked at it, having a meltdown was better than having an explosion. It was so much quieter and less messy, and she was able to keep it to herself. Gathering her composure, she walked to the cabinet, took out four yellow mugs and poured the cocoa mixture into them.

"Okay, girls," Sam said, turning his attention away from Amanda and concentrating on his two daughters. "It's already past your bedtime. So drink up, okay?" Then he pulled out a bar stool and sat down across from them.

"Amanda, sit wight here," Sara said, patting the top of the empty stool between herself and Caroline. "We saved it for you."

Amanda was so touched by the gesture, a lump swelled in her throat. "Thank you," she replied. "I would be delighted."

A moment later Amanda beamed as she took her special place at the breakfast bar. Caroline began to tell her about her day at school. The little girl grew excited when she talked about playtime and the picture she had colored of a big Tom Turkey. It reminded both Sam and Amanda that Thanksgiving was fast approaching and gave them a topic of discussion.

"Are you going someplace special for Thanksgiving Day?" he asked.

"No. I usually take calls."

"You're kidding. Every year?" he asked.

"That's right," Amanda replied.

"Don't you have any family?"

"No. I was an only child and my parents are dead."

"How about friends?"

"Of course, I have friends," she said defensively. "But that doesn't mean I have to spend Thanksgiving Day with them, does it?"

"Come to our house," Caroline piped in. "Daddy's going to cook us a big turkey. Huh, Daddy?"

Sam stood and cleared his throat. It was obvious to Amanda that he was trying to get away without addressing Caroline's invitation. A moment later, he said, "Let's go, girls."

Just like that.

Suddenly, he couldn't wait to get away from her.

The girls looked thoroughly disappointed.

Amanda was crushed. Of course, she would never allow him to see that she was.

That was what she hated about letting herself get involved with other people. The chance of getting hurt was always there.

But could she have stopped herself this time?

She glanced at Caroline and Sara—and then at their father.

Unfortunately, the answer was no.

"Can I come back to your house?" Caroline asked.

"Of course, if your dad says it's okay," Amanda replied, her heart in her throat. In spite of it, she reached out and stroked Caroline's hair.

"Can I come back, too?" Sara asked.

Glancing at Sam, Amanda held his gaze. "I'd like that very much, Sara, but again, it's up to your dad."

Sam cleared his throat. "Okay, girls, that's enough," he said, helping them put on their coats and then hurrying them toward the door. "There's something you need to understand. Dr. Lucas is a very busy lady."

That, she is, Amanda thought to herself. And until this very moment, she had convinced herself that she liked it just fine that way. Only now she found that she would have liked nothing more than to spend time with Sam's daughters. And yet, there was something very critical in all of this that she had to remember. Sam made the rules where his girls were concerned, and he obviously was very careful about who he allowed them to spend time with. Still, how could she turn her back on them when she knew they had lost their mother?

Squaring her shoulders, she gazed up at Sam. "Look," she said. "I am very busy. But maybe I can set aside some time soon for the girls to come over for a visit."

"I'd rather you didn't make any promises to my kids that you don't plan to keep," Sam said rather gruffly.

"I—I would never do such a thing," she exclaimed indignantly.

"My girls have already had more than their share of disappointments in the past year."

"I know what they're going through. I lost my mother when I was young."

"Yeah, well, don't get too close, Doc. They're not some charity case, if that's what you're thinking."

"That wasn't what I was thinking at all," she said, shocked.

"Don't think I haven't noticed something about your house. I haven't seen a single picture anywhere. Why is that, Doc? Are you too busy to have people in your life?"

Amanda drew in a sudden breath. Now, that had hurt. But she would be damned before she would let him know it. "That's none of your business."

His hands went to his hips. "In fact, if you like kids so much, why aren't you married with some of your own?"

Now that really, really hurt.

The man had no idea what he was asking. Once it had been her life's dream. Nowadays, it was simply her deepest heartache. "My career is my life," she said in self-defense, and the truth of the statement saddened her.

"Exactly my point. I know you mean well, but please don't make any promises to my kids. Understood?"

Amanda returned the heated glare he was giving her. After a moment, she bent down and gave both his daughters a big hug. "Bye now, girls," she said, swallowing back the sudden lump in her throat. But after what their father had just said to her, she wasn't about to show her emotions.

Unfortunately, she didn't completely succeed.

Sam couldn't help but notice the way Amanda was gazing at his girls. She had that same pained, faraway look in her eyes that she'd had earlier that day, right after she had delivered Lucy's baby safely into the world. It was a look of total vulnerability...almost as if she had suffered her own share of misery at some point in her life. Somehow, he was touched by it.

"Thank you for the cocoa," Caroline said politely, and the sound of his daughter's soft voice jarred Sam back into the moment.

"Me, too," Sara replied with a grin. Then, glancing at her father, she added, "Daddy, can Amanda come to my birthday pawty?"

Taken by surprise, Sam was at a complete loss for words. "Uh…we'll have to talk about it later, honey."

Sara frowned, but she didn't say anything.

After taking a deep breath, Amanda leveled her eyes on Sam. "Look, in spite of things, thanks for helping me tonight," she said.

He shrugged nonchalantly. "Don't mention it. I'd have done the same for anyone."

Amanda didn't have any delusions about that. "Yes, I'm sure you would have," she said stiffly.

A few moments later Sam helped his kids into his truck, climbed in himself and drove away, leaving Amanda standing at the door, feeling angry and somewhat confused as to what had just happened between them. One minute the guy was practically all over her at the kitchen stove, and the next he was practically accusing her of being an insensitive human being.

Just who in the hell did he think he was, anyway?

Stepping inside her house, Amanda shut the door and locked it. Well, she had known all along—hadn't she?—that Sam Arquette was going to be nothing but trouble. But had that stopped her from inviting him into her home? Oh, no, not her. Well, from now on, she planned to keep her distance from him at all costs. The hard part about that was knowing she would have to keep her distance from Caroline and Sara, as well.

But what choice did she have? Because if ever she sensed a heartbreak waiting to happen, she need look no further than Sam Arquette.

Sam called Josie Wentworth as soon as he got the girls to bed that night. She sounded surprised to be hearing from him so soon.

"You've got something, Sam?" she asked excitedly, getting right to the point.

"Unfortunately, no. At least, nothing concrete."

"Did you talk to the doctor?"

"Yes. I went to see her personally."

"And…"

"And she refuses to tell me anything about Sabrina Jensen. Apparently, she believes strongly in the doctor-patient confidentiality doctrine. She wouldn't budge an inch."

"Mmm…" Josie uttered. "Why didn't you use some ol' special forces technique on her?"

"I keep asking myself the same question," Sam replied. "I guess 'cause I was trying to be a nice guy."

Josie laughed lightly. "That's a first."

"All right, now, Josie. Be nice."

Josie sighed deeply into the receiver. "You know, don't you, Sam, that we're getting nowhere fast in our search for Sabrina Jensen."

"I know. But we'll get a break soon. You'll see."

"I hope for Jack's sake, we do. I know he would want us to find her."

"I know he would, too," Sam replied with a heaviness in his chest. "I really miss the guy, you know. He was my best friend. We went through a lot together."

"I know," Josie replied, a catch in her voice. "Sam, if you were in my shoes, what would you do next to try to find Sabrina?"

Sam grew thoughtful. Finally, he said, "I guess I would contact the authorities and ask them to put out an APB on her throughout the state. If you have a photo of her, it would be even more helpful."

"There was a snapshot among Jack's effects," Josie said, hope in her voice. "I'll check into things. In the meantime, if you happen to meet up with that doctor again, tell her I said no hard feelings about Sabrina. She has her own loyalties. I have to respect that."

"Yeah," Sam said gruffly. "I guess we do. How's Max?"

"Oh, Sam, he's wonderful."

"Sounds like you're in love. I'm happy for you, Josie."

"I know you are," she replied.

They spoke awhile longer, hanging up only after

Josie promised to keep Sam updated on any new developments.

Finally, Sam was ready to turn in for the night. But soon he realized that he wasn't going to just drop off to sleep as he had planned. Much to his regret, he kept thinking about Amanda...about how she could infuriate him at a moment's notice. And yet, something about her simply wouldn't let go of him. It was crazy...insane...mind-boggling.

Not that he was *really* interested in Amanda Lucas. It was just that she had a way of messing with his head. Not to mention his libido. It was that alluring voice of hers. It was driving him plumb mad.

So, okay. He was an idiot.

What he needed to do was get out of bed and go for a long, grueling jog.

But he didn't get out of bed. It was late, and he was tired. Besides, the girls were asleep, and he never left them alone inside the house. Eventually, he fell asleep, only to dream of Amanda. And the details of his dream were so erotic that when he awakened finally, he discovered he'd broken out in a sweat.

Much later, he dozed back off.

By the time morning arrived, Sam was determined to put Amanda completely out of his thoughts. He got Caroline off to school and then he and Sara went outside so he could do his farming chores. At lunchtime he fixed Sara a peanut butter and jelly sandwich and then put her down for a nap while he did some minor household cleaning. Sara woke up at three o'clock and soon afterward Caroline got off the school bus in front of their house. It wasn't too long before Sam decided to call it a day. He prepared a light supper for them and then cleaned up the kitchen. The problem was, the moment he found himself idle, he also found himself thinking of Amanda and about how frustrated he'd become since meeting her.

Finally, he settled down for the evening in his recliner in the den. He always helped Caroline with her homework, and tonight Sara wanted his help to make a list of friends to invite to her fourth birthday party on Saturday. Most of them were from her Sunday school class.

"Daddy," Sara said, looking up at him. "Can we invite Amanda? Pwease…"

Sam grimaced. For heaven's sake, this whole Amanda Lucas thing was out of control. He'd spoken to the woman only twice in his life—his kids, only once—but now it seemed he couldn't get her untangled from their lives.

Well, he wanted her untangled. Sara was too young to understand. He was only trying to protect her and her sister. The three of them didn't need a woman in their lives. He might not have been there for them in the past, but he was here now. He wasn't the perfect Mr. Mom, but he was getting pretty darn good at the job. Besides, he owed his wife. She had always said he spent too much time away from them. Unfortunately, it had taken her death to make him realize she was right.

Sam shook his head. "I don't think that's such a good idea, dumpling," he said, gazing at Sara. "Remember, Dr. Lucas is a very busy lady. More than likely, she'll be too busy to come."

"Pwease, Daddy. She'll come. I know she will," Sara persisted.

Sam smiled gingerly at her. "But I don't want you to be disappointed, Sara, if she doesn't."

"I won't be," the little girl replied. "Can't we invite her?"

Sam glanced at Caroline who was sitting on the floor, her schoolbooks spread out around her. "She'll come," the child said, echoing her younger sister's remark. "Amanda's nice."

The woman was infuriating—even when she wasn't around, Sam thought. But he couldn't very well say that to his young child. Instead, he sighed heavily. This conversation simply wasn't going the way he had planned. It was time he gently busted Sara and Caroline's bubble concerning Amanda.

Then why, he wondered, did he feel like the bad guy here when all he was really trying to do was protect his children from a woman who put her career above all else? A woman who, undoubtedly, would make a lousy wife and stepmother—if he was even looking for such a person. Which, of course, he wasn't.

Glancing at his girls, he saw they were staring at him, waiting on his answer.

He sighed heavily. Ah, the heck with it. Why was he fighting them, anyway? He couldn't always shelter them from the realities of life. They would see for themselves what kind of person Amanda Lucas really was when she didn't show up for Sara's party. But, even with that thought in mind, there was a part of him that secretly hoped she would prove him wrong about her. "Oh, all right," he said. "Go ahead. Invite her. We'll see what happens."

"Yippy!" Sara cried out. "She'll come, Daddy. You'll see."

But, despite his initial rejection, Sam found his blood was pulsing through his veins at the mere prospect of seeing Amanda again.

Maybe, he grumbled to himself, it wasn't just his kids he was trying to protect, after all.

Late Tuesday afternoon, Amanda was sitting behind her desk, getting ready to leave her office to make evening rounds at the hospital when she noticed a small envelope that her receptionist had placed in an upright position against her telephone. The envelope was addressed to Dr. Amanda Lucas and marked personal on the left-hand corner. She opened it and began to read. Much to her surprise, it was an invitation to Sara Arquette's birthday party on Saturday.

Amanda's first thought was that it would be better for everyone concerned if she just didn't go. After the disastrous other night, she wouldn't feel comfortable in Sam's company. For all she knew, it would be just like him to invite her to come to a party and then stand there and glare at her the whole time. Thanks, but no thanks. She would send Sara a present. That was the best she could do.

Amanda turned toward the trash can next to her desk and started to throw the invitation away. But she simply couldn't bring herself to do it. Instead, she carefully slipped it back into its envelope and placed it back in an upright position against her telephone.

And the very last thing she did before leaving her office to make hospital rounds was to glance once again at the invitation. No, she wasn't going. She simply wasn't.

Chapter Four

But it wasn't the end of the story for Amanda. For the next two days she continued to think about the invitation sitting on her desk. Maybe she was wrong. Maybe she should just forget about Sam's attitude toward her and go to the party for Sara's sake. She hated the thought of disappointing the child. Still, she had her pride. It was bad enough that Sam thought she was insensitive, but his behavior and his unguarded remark the other day about wanting to have a son were proof positive that a man like him would never want her. Why take the chance of getting hurt again? Without a doubt, it was in her own best interest to stay as far away as possible from him.

Which meant, of course, that she would have to

stay away from his kids, too. Once again, she was at loggerheads.

I'm truly sorry, Sara, Amanda thought, a sudden heaviness settling at the center of her chest. But with the Thanksgiving and Christmas holidays just around the corner, she didn't need another painful reminder that, when it came right down to it, she was all alone in this old world.

On Saturday morning, the day of Sara's birthday party, Amanda awoke with a start. Instantly realizing that she had been caught in the clutches of a recurring nightmare, she rolled over on her back and lay there momentarily, staring at the ceiling overhead. A lump swelled in her throat. The nightmare was the product of something that had happened to her over ten years ago. Even now, the memory of her ex-fiancé's rejection when he'd discovered that she was infertile still could cause her pain.

Their wedding had been less than a month away and Amanda had been trying very hard to make sure every little detail was taken care of. She'd found that her fiancé was a stickler for perfection. One evening, after she'd arranged a doctor's visit to go over the results of some tests she had taken during a comprehensive physical, she was to meet her fiancé at his office.

The test results turned out to be devastating. Her

doctor told her that she had a severe case of en-
dometriosis and that she would never be able to
conceive children. Needing the comfort and support of her fiancé, she had rushed to his office with
the tragic news. Instead of comfort, she had gotten
his complete rejection.

"How could you keep something like this from
me for all this time?" he had said angrily, as
though her condition was something she had secretly planned to keep from him until now. Which,
of course, wasn't the case at all. She was heartbroken…shocked…in need of a shoulder to cry on.

"I—I didn't keep this from you," she had stammered. "I just found out today. I know it's a shock,
but I need you—"

"A shock," he had retorted mockingly. "You
have no idea just what a shock this is. My father
is getting ready to make me a full partner in his
law firm. Do you know what that means? Finally,
I'll have the office right next door to his."

"That's wonderful," she had said, trying to
make sense of what he was saying. She knew how
much he wanted the office and the partnership his
father was now offering him. But why wasn't he
taking her into his arms and telling her that everything was going to be all right?

The expression on his face was so hard…so
cold.

"You know what that means, don't you?" he

had repeated. "It means that one day I'll want to make my own son a partner."

"We could always adopt," she had said through her tears. She was still in shock, and just so bewildered at the change in him.

"That's absurd," he had stated. "My father will never accept a grandchild that isn't his blood. I can't marry you now. I have an obligation to my family."

"But I thought you loved me," Amanda had said.

"And I thought you could give me a son," he had replied evenly, without even the slightest sound of remorse in his tone of voice.

"Is that the only reason you were marrying me?"

"I strive for perfection, Amanda. You know that."

"And I'm not perfect anymore. Is that what you're saying?"

"I'm saying that any man in my shoes would do the same thing. And if you don't believe me, just ask around," he had replied.

As if she would have ever done such a thing. Instead, she had created a cocoon of protection. To this day, she still lived in it.

Amanda finally got up from bed, dressed and headed for the hospital to make her morning rounds. Upon arriving, she poured herself a cup of coffee that smelled and looked as if it had been brewed hours ago. She took a sip and grimaced. She was right. It tasted awful. Turning, she threw the full cup in a nearby trash can and then selected a bottle of orange juice from the vending machine right next to the coffeepot.

Suddenly, without even the slightest warning, Sara and Caroline's sweet little faces flashed through Amanda's mind. The two little girls were probably awake by now and getting all excited about Sara's birthday party later that day. And then Amanda pictured Sam in the kitchen baking Sara's cake, and she couldn't help herself. She had to smile. Because not even in her wildest dreams did that scene fit her image of him. Sam was too much a man's man to be that domesticated. He was an ex-soldier, for heaven's sake. He was simply too sexy. She could picture him out in his yard chopping wood, but not in his kitchen decorating a four-year-old's birthday cake.

Realizing how easily Sam and his children had slipped into her thoughts, Amanda turned and started down the hall toward one of her patient's rooms. Halfway there, she stopped short.

Oh, for heaven's sake, she had forgotten to send Sara a birthday present as she'd planned. Thoroughly upset with herself, Amanda remained frozen for a long moment before she realized that she still had time to get a gift to the child before the party started. She walked straight to the doctor's lounge where she knew there was a telephone. She looked up the number for the children's clothing shop down on Main Street and dialed it. The store clerk who answered was very helpful and promised to take care of everything, including the delivery. After completing the call, Amanda went back to making her rounds, relieved that she had remembered in time. She would have been heartsick if she hadn't.

After seeing her patients, Amanda headed straight for her office. Her desk was piled with business letters that needed tending to. Not only that, but she wanted to pull Sabrina Jensen's file and review it. Who knew, maybe it held a clue to the young woman's whereabouts.

Soon she was seated in the plush leather chair behind her desk, Sabrina's file placed in front of her. She saw the invitation that Sara had sent to her still placed against her telephone. She didn't reach for it, though. But then, she didn't need to. She'd already read it so many times, she knew it by heart.

Right next to it was a note from Kathy reminding her once again about the puppies her niece was giving away. Kathy was convinced that Amanda needed a pet and had been leaving her notes to that effect for a couple of weeks now. However, with her odd hours, Amanda was just as convinced that a pet was the last thing she needed.

Taking a deep breath, she opened Sabrina Jensen's file and began to study the paperwork inside. Amanda already knew that the only information in the file that wasn't bogus was Sabrina's name, and possibly her date of birth, and the fact that her last known mailing address was The Single C, a prominent spread in Muskogee County, owned by her cousin, Max Carter. But she dialed the telephone number Sabrina had given anyway, and waited to see what would happen. Sure enough, a recording came on, saying that the number had been disconnected.

Not for the first time, Amanda speculated about her patient's suspicious disappearance. She knew, of course, that Sabrina was an expectant mother. And from her experience with other pregnant women—and, of course, from her own basic instincts—she knew that if Sabrina thought for a second that her unborn child was in some kind of jeopardy, from the Wentworths or whomever, she would do anything to protect him. Even if that meant running from the very people who said they wanted to help. In any case, Sabrina was undoubtedly frightened and alone, and Amanda was worried about her, both as a doctor and as a woman. But at the same time, even as she sat in the comfort and safety of her office, she knew she would trade places with Sabrina in a heartbeat. She thought again of her young patient carrying the child of the man she loved. As far as Amanda was concerned, nothing—absolutely nothing in life—could possibly ever equal that kind of joy.

Finally, after looking through Sabrina's entire file, Amanda realized there were no clues to the young woman's whereabouts. Apparently, Sabrina had been very careful not to leave behind a paper trail that could be followed. Closing the file, Amanda sat back in her leather chair and gave the matter some more thought. Eventually, she placed Sabrina's file to the side and went to work on the pile of mail stacked on her desk.

Time passed. Amanda glanced at her wristwatch. Two o'clock. Instinctively she found herself thinking that Sara's party would be starting in an hour. And no matter how hard she tried to rationalize the need to stay away, there was something deeply disturbing to her about missing it.

And then, like clockwork, Amanda's thoughts of Sara naturally conjured up the child's father.

The truth of the matter was, Sam was the only reason she wasn't going to Sara's birthday. He was arrogant and intimidating, and he made her feel so damned vulnerable. For years now she had fought so hard to deal with her feelings of inadequacy as a woman, only to have him come along and toss the truth right back in her face. And now she knew.

She wasn't dealing with her feelings. They were still there beneath the covering of her skin, lurking…hiding…threatening to shatter her confidence in herself without a moment's warning.

No way could she continue to let that happen.

Amanda found it useless to try to sit in her office and open any more letters. She decided that she couldn't take the turmoil going on inside her any longer. In one swift move she slammed the letter opener down on top of her desk and stood. Dammit, this was ridiculous. Deep down inside, she wanted to go to Sara's birthday party. And, frankly, she would be a complete fool if she let fear stop her from doing so. To hell with Sam Arquette and the way he made her feel inside. She was going to that party because she wanted to— not because of him.

So now that she had made that decision, it seemed imperative that she do something special for Sara—and for Caroline, too. Something that would make Sam's two little daughters remember her fondly. No doubt this would be her only chance to do something special for them. She had a feeling that Sam wasn't likely to be inviting her back to his home anytime soon. Picking up Kathy's note about the puppies, Amanda knew exactly what she was going to do. She called Kathy and made arrangements to pick up one within the hour. Then she rushed home to get ready, giving extra attention to her hair and makeup. After all, she was going to a party. She wanted to look her best.

For Sara's and Caroline's sakes, of course.

After all, all their friends would be there.

Within forty-five minutes she was heading out of town for the Arquette farm with a brand-new doghouse in her trunk and a six-week-old puppy asleep on her lap.

Amanda was going to her first birthday party in years, and she could hardly wait to get there.

Sam Arquette glanced at his wristwatch for the hundredth time. It was three-fifteen and Sara's birthday party had started. It looked as though Amanda Lucas wasn't going to come, after all. Somewhere deep inside he had known all along that she wouldn't. Frankly, he could have cared less. He just hoped she was happy living her life as a loner. Sara and Caroline were going to be the ones disappointed when they realized that she wasn't coming, and he hated to see that happen to them.

And, okay, if the truth be known, maybe he was a little disappointed, too.

But only a little.

And only because of his girls.

Actually, he had other, more immediate problems to worry about right now. Mrs. Cunningham was having back trouble again—a condition that had required strict bed rest several times in the past year that he'd known her—yet she had insisted on coming today to help him with Sara's party, and he was trying to make sure she didn't overwork herself.

Looking up, Sam saw Sara running across the yard toward him and groaned out loud. He already knew what she was planning to ask him. Unfortunately, his answer wasn't going to be to her liking.

"Daddy," she said breathlessly, coming to a stop right in front of him. "Is Amanda coming?"

Sam shook his head. "I don't think so, dumplin'. She would've been here by now."

Sara frowned. "Oh," she said. The letdown showing on her face tore at Sam's heart. Dropping her gaze, she turned and walked away.

"Damn you, Amanda," Sam muttered to himself as he whirled around to go into the house. Instead, he ran smack dab into Mrs. Cunningham who was just coming out the door.

"Damn who?" she asked teasingly.

"Dr. Lucas, that's who," he replied.

"W-what did she do?" Mrs. Cunningham asked, furrowing her brow.

"The girls wanted me to invite her to come today, so I did. But she didn't show—just like I knew she wouldn't."

"Maybe she's delivering a baby," Mrs. Cunningham said.

"Yeah, maybe," Sam replied with a slight smirk. "But she could've called," he added, before going inside the house to get what he needed from the kitchen. When he came back outside, he saw that Sara, Caroline and the other children at the party were all gathered around someone. A second later he saw who that someone was.

"Well, I'll be," he said under his breath. "She came after all." Suddenly, something in his gut pulled hard. It was brief, but powerful. And that was when Sam first realized that where the good doctor was concerned, he just might be heading for more trouble than he could ever imagine. But, deciding to ignore such a thought, he strolled with a deliberate gait toward them.

By this time, Sara had already run up to Amanda and taken something from her. Now his little birthday girl was running across the backyard toward him, with Caroline close at her heels. "Daddy, Daddy," Sara called out. "Look what Amanda brought us. It's a puppy."

Sam glanced down at the ball of short black fur with two dark eyes, and then lifted his gaze to Amanda's face. Giving him a sheepish grin, she said, "I hope you don't mind."

Sam noticed right away that Amanda's complexion looked flush—radiant. Her shiny brown hair glowed in the late autumn sun, and the pink cashmere sweater and pants outfit she wore fit her slender curves to a *T*. The bottom line was, she looked a whole lot different from the other day in her office.

A whole lot different.

He liked the change.

After examining the happy faces of his two children, he said, "Do I have a choice?"

Amanda shrugged. "I guess not. Sorry. I suppose I should have asked you first."

"You probably should have, but it's all right. I happen to like dogs," he said with a grin.

Amanda grinned back. "Yeah, you look like the type who would."

"Do I, now?" he said, widening his smile. Suddenly the woman he had thought was an iceberg no longer seemed as cold. It was her smile, he thought. It made all the difference in the world.

"Can we keep the puppy, Daddy? Can we?" Caroline asked,

Sam drew in a deep breath. "Yes, honey, you can keep the puppy."

"By the way," Amanda said carefully, "there's a doghouse in the trunk of my car. I could use some help getting it out."

Sam's gaze locked with hers. "Sure."

Amanda led the way to her car with Sam fast approaching at her heels. She made it to her car and opened the trunk while all she could think about was the fact that he was practically breathing down her neck the whole time.

Sam took one look at the doghouse and said, "I can get this out by myself."

"No," Amanda replied. "I insist on helping you."

Sam shrugged. "Fine with me," he said with a grin. Then he motioned toward the trunk. "Be my guest."

"Well, if you'll get that end, I'll get this one," Amanda said, gesturing.

Sam immediately reached inside the trunk and grabbed his end of the doghouse. Amanda watched and then grabbed hold of her side. "On the count of three," she said, "we'll lift it out and place it on the ground."

Sam nodded, amused. "I'm ready when you are."

"One...two...three." Amanda lifted her end of the doghouse. It was a piece of cake. Well, maybe not exactly. She was straining somewhat. But then, she was in such an awkward position and the dog-house was so much heavier than she thought....

"Put it down," Sam instructed.

He had already placed his end on the ground and was standing with his hands on his hips, laughing at her. In the next second, though, he was behind her, helping her with her end. Together, they got it to the ground.

"Well, now," Amanda said, releasing a deep breath. "That wasn't so tough, after all." When she turned around, she found herself facing Sam. Her breathing was still rapid and her cheeks were undoubtedly still flushed from her struggle with the doghouse. Both conditions only got worse when she realized that his arms were now encircling her waist.

"Thanks for coming, Doc. The puppy was a great idea. I wish I had thought of it myself. You have a special way with my girls," he said, grinning at her.

"I'm glad," she said, her voice growing husky. His grin widened.

"Have I mentioned to you that I love the sound of your voice," he said.

Amanda's breath caught in her throat. "No, I don't think so."

"Well, I do."

"Really?" she replied, swallowing hard.

"Uh-huh," he said. Then he leaned forward and smelled her skin just behind her earlobe. "And you smell good, too."

"Sam…" Amanda whispered in a sort of panicky voice.

"Shh," he replied, placing his finger over her lips. "Tell me something, Doc," he said, his voice growing husky and deep. He barely touched her arms as he ran his hands slowly down the sleeves of her sweater. Looking deep into her eyes, he said, "Do you always run away when someone tries to get close to you?"

Amanda gaped. "Of course, not," she replied.

Sam grinned. "I'm glad to hear you say that," he replied, suddenly pulling her closer. "'Cause I'm going to kiss you now."

Then before she could offer rebuttal, he leaned forward and covered her lips with his.

At first, she was too stunned to respond. But when Sam deepened his kiss to a passionate assault, she couldn't resist any longer. Her arms went around his neck. And for one timeless second, nothing mattered but the two of them.

But then, suddenly, the kiss ended and Amanda broke free of his embrace. Shaken, she began to smooth out her clothing. "I can't believe you did that," she said. "Worse, I can't believe I let you."

"Okay, so we lost control for a moment. No big deal."

Amanda narrowed her eyes. "I knew it would be a mistake for me to come here today."

"Oh?" he said with a shake of his head. "So you thought of not coming, did you?"

"I came for Sara's sake. And, of course, for Caroline's, too."

"Frankly, I'm surprised that you considered their feelings."

"I'm not surprised you said that," she said. "You've obviously made up your mind about the kind of person you think I am."

Stiffening her shoulders, she headed back in the direction of the birthday party, leaving the doghouse behind for Sam to see about. After all, he had said he could handle it himself, so why not let him.

Amanda spent the next hour of Sara's birthday party deliberately avoiding Sam—which wasn't all that difficult to do since he and Mrs. Cunningham were busy cutting cake and passing out cups of punch. She wanted to offer her help, but she didn't think Sam would accept it. Instead, she played with Sara and Caroline and their friends. Actually, other than that one brief—though electrically charged—encounter with Sam upon her arrival, she was having a good time. It was a gorgeous day. The sun was shining, and the air was crisp and cool. Everywhere she looked, there were signs that winter was fast approaching. Thanksgiving, she knew, would be upon them before she knew it. Suddenly, she was overcome by a feeling of melancholy. It always happened to her during this time of year. Maybe because her mother had died in the fall. Or maybe because fall reminded her of how alone she was in the world.

Faintly, Amanda became aware that someone was saying her name and her morose thoughts slipped from her mind. She whirled around and found Sam standing just a few feet behind her. He smiled. "A penny for your thoughts?" he said.

In spite of herself, Amanda smiled. "I'll take nothing less than a dime."

Sam dug in his jean pocket and came out with a handful of change. He reached for a coin and then flicked it up into the air. Automatically, Amanda caught it. When she opened her hand, she found a dime.

Her smile widened, and then he smiled, too.

"Come on," he said, stepping alongside her and placing his hand at the small of her back. "It's time for cake and punch."

What was it about this man that she couldn't seem to resist, no matter how hard she tried? Was it the way one glance from him could start a fire burning in her? Regardless, she couldn't let this continue to happen. Otherwise, she had little doubt that she was going to regret it.

Sam steered them to a place where they had a perfect view of Sara opening her gifts. The little girl was thrilled with the dress Amanda had had delivered. However, Amanda was still glad that she had brought Sara and Caroline the puppy, too. She was also pleased that their father had approved.

At some point in all the excitement of eating

cake and having Sara open her gifts, Mrs. Cunningham came up to Sam with a pained look on her face. "Sam, it's my back. It's giving me trouble. I'm gonna have to go home."

Sam took hold of the older woman's arm. "I knew this was going to happen if you came today. I'm taking you home right now and putting you to bed. And you're going to stay there. That's an order."

"Why don't I take her home?" Amanda suggested. "You have the party to tend to."

"He's gonna need some help cleaning up," Mrs. Cunningham said. "Would you mind coming back to help him?"

"I—uh—sure," Amanda replied. And she meant it. She certainly didn't mind helping anyone out.

"Look, I won't need any help, okay?" Sam said.

"Nonsense," Mrs. Cunningham replied. "Now, you know you're gonna need some help. Dr. Lucas will do just fine."

Amanda turned to face Sam. "If you'd rather that I not come back…"

"But, of course, he wants you to come back," Mrs. Cunningham replied. "He's just like every other man I know. He's simply too proud to say it."

Sam rolled his eyes at his neighbor. "I can never win with you," he said.

Mrs. Cunningham looked at Amanda. "You'll come back to help him, then, won't you?"

Amanda glanced over at Sam and shrugged. "Of course," she replied.

Sam helped Mrs. Cunningham walk to Amanda's car, so Amanda could drive the older woman to her home which was a good country-block down the road. "Make sure she goes straight to bed," he said to Amanda.

She looked him squarely in the face. "I'm a doctor, remember?"

Heaven help him, Sam thought, but there was something about this woman that made him crazy inside—crazy like he'd never been in his whole life. If he didn't know better, he would think he was losing it.

But, of course, he knew better.

Perhaps what he really needed was a night out on the town.

Yeah, he thought to himself, that was exactly what he needed.

And soon.

One way or another, he was going to get rid of this crazy obsession he had of Amanda Lucas, if it was the last thing he ever did.

He had wanted a challenge. Well, now it was time he did something about it.

Chapter Five

Sam glanced at his wristwatch again. It was forty-five minutes now since Amanda had left the party to take Mrs. Cunningham home. He was thinking of calling to see what was keeping her so long. The only thing stopping him was the idea that maybe she had left a long time ago. If he called and she wasn't there, he'd look like a complete fool in Mrs. Cunningham's eyes.

He had suspected all along that Amanda wasn't going to come back. She had just feigned agreement to please Mrs. Cunningham. He was getting to know Amanda well enough now to realize that she was the kind of woman who never gave an inch. At least, not where he was concerned, anyway.

Indeed, she was stubborn.

And willful.

And sexy as all get-out.

She acted all toughlike, but he was beginning to wonder if it wasn't just an act in order to cover up a past hurt. He had seen that faraway look in her eyes, the one that made her look so vulnerable. Had the love of her life dumped her? For some reason he wished he knew. She was such an added complication in his life. His days—and nights— would be a lot simpler right now if he was attracted to someone less complicated than she. But then again, it wasn't just anyone who could intrigue him.

At four-thirty the last of Sara's friends left the party. Sara and Caroline helped Sam bring Sara's gifts into the house while the puppy Amanda had given them slept soundly in one corner of the kitchen on a makeshift bed of old towels. Sam started taking down the decorations in the backyard. He was deep in thought when a voice behind him said, "Hi. Am I too late to help?" There wasn't another voice on earth that affected him like hers. He turned and saw Amanda standing just a few feet away, and his whole system shut down. It was as though someone had momentarily pulled the plug on him. Finally, though, he was able to pull himself together.

"I didn't think you were coming back."

"I had an emergency phone call while I was at Mrs. Cunningham's," she said, stepping forward to help him finish taking down the decorations. Already, Sam could smell the light floral scent of her fragrance.

"Was Mrs. Cunningham all right when you left her?"

"She was in bed. Before leaving her house, I heated her a bowl of soup and made sure the telephone was within her reach. She should be fine for now. I plan to check on her later."

"I'm planning to do that, too," he replied.

Amanda suddenly stopped what she was doing. "Sam—look—I've been thinking about something. I'd like to clear the air with you about the other day when you came into my office and asked about Sabrina Jensen. I want you to understand that I was only doing what I thought was best for Sabrina. First of all, I didn't know you from Adam and certainly had no way of knowing if the story you were giving me was true."

Sam nodded. "I realize that now. I should have given you the facts and then waited for you to verify them."

"That would've helped. Since I've gotten to know you better, my feelings about the matter have changed somewhat."

"Really?"

"Well, let's just say I now trust you enough to

tell you what I know about Sabrina.'' Amanda took a deep breath. ''Look, she was my patient, but I haven't seen her in a while. She missed her last appointment and when my staff tried to reach her to reschedule, they discovered that the address and telephone number she had given for her file were phony. I haven't heard from her since, and I don't know where she is.''

''Why was she coming to you?''

''I can't divulge that kind of information.''

Sam narrowed his eyes. ''Was she pregnant?''

''Look, I'm trying to tell you as much as I can without compromising my oath as a doctor.''

For several intense moments, Sam gazed at her long and hard. Finally, though, he shook his head in understanding. ''The Wentworths won't give up until they find her.''

''I'm glad to know that,'' Amanda replied. ''Someone needs to be there for her. I'd like to know when they find her.''

Sam gave her a surprised look. ''Sure. And, Amanda, thanks.'' His smile was warm and genuine, and together they returned to cleaning up the mess from the party in companionable silence.

But for Amanda, thoughts of Sabrina out there somewhere pregnant and alone weren't that easy to dispense with. At least, in the next few months, Sabrina would have her baby to comfort her. Amanda had no one.

Suddenly, her eyes filled with tears.

"Hey, what's wrong?" Sam asked almost immediately, taking her by the shoulders and turning her around to face him. "Why the tears?"

"It's nothing," Amanda said, a slight tremor in her voice.

But Sam pulled her against him anyway, hugging her tight to his chest. "Come on, you can tell me what's wrong," he said, sounding sincere. "Is it something I said?"

Amanda burrowed her face in his chest. "No," she replied. "It's nothing, really. It's been a busy week. I'm just tired."

"Tired?" Sam replied with a chuckle. "Do you always cry like this when you're tired?"

Somehow, Amanda managed to lift her head and give him a weak smile. "No, thank goodness," she replied. "It's nothing, really," she repeated.

"Well, if you say so," he said, still holding her close. "Everything is going to work out all right," he replied, his arms still wrapped around her.

Amanda had never in her life felt so safe...so secure.

The spell was broken, however, when Caroline suddenly appeared beside them. "Daddy," she said, her eyes widening in surprise when she saw Amanda in his arms. "What's wrong with Amanda?" she asked.

At the sound of the child's voice, Amanda

sprang away from Sam. "Nothing's wrong with me, honey," she replied. "I had something in my eye and your daddy was trying to help me get it out."

"Oh," Caroline replied, apparently accepting her answer. Then she glanced at her father. "Daddy, me and Sara want to know if we're still having hot dogs for supper."

Sam coughed self-consciously. "Yeah, pumpkin, we sure are," he replied.

"Is Amanda staying?"

"Uh—well, she can if she wants to," he answered.

"Do you want to, Amanda? Please..." Caroline asked.

"W-well, honey, it's not that I don't want to. It's just that—well, I'll have to check with my answering service first."

"There's a phone you can use in the kitchen," Sam said.

"Thanks," she replied in awe of what was happening. Was Sam trying to rush her to use the telephone in the hopes that she wouldn't be able to stay for supper, or was he just trying to be nice?

Just because he had offered her a moment of comfort didn't mean anything. He probably couldn't wait for her to leave.

Once inside the house, she used the phone in the kitchen to dial her answering service and was told that she didn't have any calls. Surprised, she hung up and mused aloud, "Well, what do you know? Everything is quiet on the hospital front."

"I hope you like hot dogs," Sam said, carrying in an armload of party favors and dumping them on one corner of the kitchen table.

Amanda still wasn't sure whether he truly wanted her to stay or not.

"Look," she said self-consciously. "I think I'll be going, anyway."

"Why?" he asked. "The kids'll love it if you stay for supper. Just don't expect too much on the table. Hot dogs at my house consists of wieners, canned chili and, sometimes, day-old buns."

"What...no mustard?"

Sam gave her a blank stare. Finally, though, he seemed to catch on that she was joking. "I just don't want you thinking it's going to be a gourmet meal or anything."

"It isn't?" she replied with just a hint of a smile on her lips.

Shaking his head, Sam laughed lightly and then went outside to get what was left of Sara's birthday cake. Returning, he said, "Well, one thing for sure, we have plenty of dessert."

"Mmm...yummy," Amanda replied. "I love cake."

"Sweets for the sweets, right?"

At that precise moment, Sam looked up and his

gaze locked with Amanda's. An instant heat rushed to her face as she remembered the way he'd held her in his strong arms only minutes before. The problem was, she had a feeling he was remembering, too. Then, just as quickly, that same heat began to spread slowly down the rest of her body.

Needing to break the spell, she quickly glanced away and said, "Where are the girls?"

"Probably in the living room watching TV."

"Need any help with supper?"

"Nope," he replied.

Amanda cleared her throat. "Well, okay, then. What do you say I go and see what the girls are up to?"

"That's a good idea. In fact, tell them to pick up the toys I'm almost positive they have scattered all over the den."

No sooner had Amanda turned to go to the living room, than the girls came running into the kitchen. "We're hungry, Daddy," Caroline said.

"I'll have supper ready in a jiffy. In the meantime, make sure you've picked up all of your toys in the den."

Both little girls hung their heads.

Amanda saw the girls' reaction. Standing a safe distance behind Sam, she decided to lighten the moment by giving Sara and Caroline a look that said, *Ain't your father a stick-in-the-mud?* She didn't mean anything by it. It was almost a spontaneous reaction. But Caroline and Sara started laughing.

Obviously dumbstruck by their reactions, Sam just stared at his kids. Finally, though, he must have gotten the hint that something was going on behind his back, and he glanced over his shoulder at Amanda. ''What are you doing?'' he asked.

''Who me?'' Amanda replied, all innocentlike. This time the girls giggled even harder.

''Yes, you,'' he said with a grin, turning suddenly and grabbing hold of Amanda. He sat in a kitchen chair and pulled her into his lap.

''I didn't do anything,'' she said, taken by surprise.

''Oh, yeah,'' he replied, laughing. ''Well, let me show you what I do to sneaky females who make funny faces behind my back.'' Then he began tickling her—mercilessly—and she squealed with laughter.

It was torture to be tickled that way.

And yet, it was wonderful.

She gasped for air.

He tickled her across her ribs, over her abdomen and all the way up to the base of her throat. Sam had such strong fingers, and they danced across her skin in a firm, yet gentle way. He was giving her more pleasure—and pain—than she could stand.

''Stop—stop,'' she gasped. ''Girls—someone—help me.''

Caroline laughed. But, apparently, Sara took Amanda's pleas to heart. "Daddy, stop," she cried out. "You're hurting Amanda."

Sam finally let go of Amanda, and she jumped to her feet and began straightening her clothing.

"Sara, honey," Sam said, "I wasn't hurting Amanda. We were just playing."

"That's right," Amanda said breathlessly. She was glad the child's confusion had put a stop to Sam's strange behavior. She couldn't have taken much more of it. But at the same time, she couldn't let Sara think that Sam was actually hurting her. Because he wasn't. She just had to get control of herself first. Her heart was pounding like mad. Her legs were trembling like a newborn colt's. In fact, she felt all discombobulated. She could just imagine what her hair looked like.

"See, Sara, honey," Sam said, smiling at his youngest daughter. "It was all playlike." Turning to Amanda, he said, "You're all right, aren't you?"

Amanda was still breathless. "Yes, of course," she replied, quickly trying to comb her hair back from her face.

With one final glance at Amanda, Sam turned and got busy with supper preparations. Amanda followed Sara and Caroline to the den and helped them pick up their scattered toys.

For the first time in years, Amanda's emotional

guards were on shaky ground. If she wasn't care-ful—which, of course, she was trying to be—she was going to find herself with one big heartache on her hands. A heartache, she now feared, that was in the making. Already Caroline and Sara had become very special to her, and she had something very basic in common with them. She, too, had had to grow up without a mother. But even though the girls had been through a lot in their young lives, they were sweet and innocent and expected abso-lutely nothing from her. Every moment with them was precious to her.

And then, of course, there was Sam. And, she supposed, he was her biggest problem of all. Since her ex-fiancé's rejection, she had never allowed a man to get close enough to her to crack the steel plate of armor she had erected around herself. But Sam hadn't asked her permission to get close. He had simply found a weakness in her armor and barged right in like the seasoned soldier he was.

Once Amanda and the girls were finished pick-ing up toys in the den, they returned to the kitchen to find Sam in the middle of preparing supper. They pitched in to help him by setting the table. Finally, they were all seated at the table, and the meal turned out to be relaxed and fun. Amanda found it amazing how eating hot dogs could bring out the kid in a person—including herself.

The girls finished and Sam excused them from

the table. "How about one more?" he said, giving her a daring grin.

"I'm stuffed," Amanda replied. "I couldn't possibly."

"Ah, come on. Just one more. It's only a hot dog."

Amanda laughed. Surprisingly, she really was enjoying herself.

Suddenly, Sam grew quiet and instinctively Amanda did, too. Then, he reached across the table with his napkin in hand and gently wiped one corner of her mouth. "You...uh...had a dab of mustard," he said, gazing into her eyes.

"Oh," Amanda replied, mesmerized by the intensity of his gaze and by the sweet way he had handled what could have been an embarrassing moment for her.

It was outrageous the way one look from this one particular man could make her feel all breathless inside. Trying to ignore her racing heart, Amanda scooted her chair back from the table. "Well, it's getting late. I should be going. Thanks for supper."

"Just my luck," Sam said with a snap of his fingers, "that you should decide to leave just when I was going to ask a favor of you."

"Oh? What kind of favor?"

Sam grinned. "Well," he said. "I was going to ask you to supervise the girls' bath while I cleaned up in the kitchen. They need supervision, otherwise they flood the bathroom floor.''

''Me?'' Amanda said.

''Yeah,'' he replied. ''Why not?''

''I've never done anything like that before.''

''Well, don't you think it's time you did? In fact, you seem to enjoy my kids so much, I have to ask again why you don't have any of your own?''

Amanda wasn't in the least bit prepared for that question, and it shook her right down to the tips of her toes. If he knew the real reason why she didn't have children, what would he think of her as a woman? ''I had to make a choice a long time ago. I chose a career.''

Liar. Fate had made that decision for her.

In fact, right at this moment she wanted kids so bad the ache was palpable. But she would never tell Sam the truth. He would only look at her with pity—or disgust. In either case, she knew she couldn't handle it.

''I'll stay long enough to supervise the girls' bath,'' she said, hoping to change the subject. After all, it was the least she could do after having stayed for supper. But then—no doubt about it—she would have to go. If she was going to salvage any part of her heart, she simply had to.

''I'll make us some coffee for afterward.''

This was her moment, Amanda thought. Just say no.

She took a deep breath. "Not tonight," she replied.

"Just one cup," he said, grinning at her.

Amanda hesitated for a moment. She felt as though she were being pulled apart. One half of her wanted to stay; the other half wanted to go. "Maybe just one," she finally said.

His grin widened. "Yeah, just one," he replied.

As soon as Amanda left the kitchen, Sam paused a moment to try to figure out what he was doing. He had vowed on his wife's grave that he would take care of their children, that nothing else in his life would ever take precedence over them. Not his job as a navy SEABEE—which was why he had retired—and especially not another woman.

And, heaven knew, he was the last man on earth who would be looking for a stepmother for his kids. He had grown up under the critical eye of a scheming stepmother who'd always managed to make him and his brother look bad to their father. And even though Amanda didn't seem that kind of person, there was no way he was ever going to take the chance of having that happen to his girls. They deserved better.

Whatever it was he wanted from Amanda Lucas, he knew one thing for sure—it was nothing permanent.

Chapter Six

Caroline and Sara were delighted when Amanda told them that she was going to supervise their bath. Giggling, they led the way down the hall and into the bathroom.

"Remember, no splashing," Sam yelled out from the kitchen.

Smiling, Amanda closed the bathroom door then turned to face the girls. "Okay," she said, "let's get started. I'll get the water going while the two of you undress."

The girls shimmied out of their clothes in no time at all. The tub was just beginning to fill up.

"Can we get in?" Sara asked.

Amanda nodded.

"Our hair," Caroline said suddenly. "Daddy always pins it up so it won't get wet."

The idea that Sam took the time to pin up his daughters' hair before they bathed set a warm feeling spiraling through Amanda.

"He uses those," Caroline continued, pointing to a small basket on a shelf above the tub. Reaching for it, Amanda saw it was filled with ribbons and hair clips of all sorts and colors. She could only gaze at them and wonder about the man who cared enough to place them there. Finally, though, she realized that Sara was talking to her.

"It's my turn to go first," she said. "Daddy says we have to take turns. Caroline was first last night to get her hair pinned up. See," she continued, pointing to the wall. "We have a chart."

Following the child's line of vision, Amanda saw a handwritten sheet of paper taped to the wall. Once again, a warm, gut-wrenching feeling sliced its way through her. *This should have been her life. Only, it wasn't. How unfair. She would have done her very best to be a good wife and mother.* "Okay, then," she said gently. "Come here, Sara, and let me pin your hair up."

It took Amanda only a few moments to get both girls' hair pinned up. By that time, the tub was half-filled.

"Can we get in?" Caroline asked.

"Sure can," Amanda replied. "Just be careful." She ended up helping Sara climb over the rim.

"Can we put bubble bath in the water?" Caroline asked.

"Oh, I don't know," Amanda replied. She glanced up at the shelf above the tub and saw a pink-and-white box that was plainly marked by the manufacturer as Bubble Bath. For just a fraction of a second, she thought to go and ask Sam if it was all right to use it, but then decided that she was supervising this bath and the decision was up to her.

"Okay," she said, reaching for the box. Opening it, she poured a small amount of granules in the palm of her hand. After smelling the strawberry fragrance, she dumped them in the tub.

"Put more than that," Caroline said. "Daddy says our water is hard."

"He does, does he?" Amanda said, grinning at the child.

"Uh-huh," Caroline replied.

Widening her grin, Amanda said, "Okay, then. Here goes." This time, she poured a generous amount of soap granules near the open faucet. Within seconds, thick layers of bubbles began to form. The girls grabbed handfuls and began blowing them into the air. Enjoying the moment, Amanda did, too. The three of them were laughing and having the best time when all of a sudden Amanda realized that the bubbles in the tub had risen more than she'd planned.

"Oh, my goodness," she said, suddenly jumping to her feet and reaching for the faucet that was now somewhere below the bubble line. Finally, she found it and quickly turned it off. But the tub was so full of water that bubbles had begun to ooze over the rim.

The girls were still giggling and blowing bubbles from the palms of their hands. They had bubbles in their hair. In fact, there were bubbles just about everywhere.

Oh-oh, Amanda thought. They were in trouble.

There was a knock at the door. A moment later, Sam opened it and stepped inside. For a second he just stood still, staring at the sight of them. Finally, though, he glanced down at Amanda. "What in the world's going on in here?"

"I—uh...I haven't the slightest idea what you mean. You asked me to supervise the girls' bath, and so I'm in the process of doing so."

"You call this supervising?" he asked, gazing around the bathroom as though in awe.

"It's really not that bad. It's just bubbles," she said, defending herself—and the girls, too.

"We're having fun, Daddy," Sara piped in with a giggle. "Can Amanda be our new mommy?"

Suddenly, the bubbles were the least of Amanda's problems.

Of all the questions for Sara to have asked. Immediately, she felt her insides lock up. If only the innocent child knew how much she wanted to be someone's mother.

"You have a mommy," Sam replied.

"Yeah, but she's in heaven and can't play with us anymore."

For one brief moment, Sam's eyes met Amanda's. She knew that Sara's question had shaken him. Of all the women in the world, undoubtedly she was the last person he would have considered being fun. She didn't even think he particularly liked her. He tolerated her because of his girls, which was just fine with her. The strange part was, the more she was around him, the more she found she admired him, both as a father and as a man. And in his own way, he was beginning to be kind of fun, too—even if at times he acted like an old fuddy-duddy.

Like now.

Sam stepped forward and knelt down at the side of the tub. "I know you miss your mommy," he said to Sara in a soothing voice. "I'm trying very hard to do the things for you that she used to do. But if I've forgotten something, all you need to do is tell me."

Suddenly, Amanda felt uncomfortable. As if she were an outsider, intruding on a private conversation. She stood and cleared her throat. "Maybe I should be going now."

"Oh, no," Sara cried out, her big eyes suddenly

filling with tears. "Don't go." She glanced at her father. "Daddy, pwease, make Amanda stay."

"Look," Sam said. "You don't have to go. The girls want you to stay. Besides, I've already made coffee."

Amanda gazed at him for a long moment. She wanted to stay with this family more than she'd ever wanted anything. "Are you sure?"

"Positive," he replied.

Amanda took a deep, steadying breath. "Okay, I'll stay," she said. Dropping back down to her knees, she picked up a washcloth and soap. "Girls, I guess we need to finish what we started."

"I can help," Sam said. "I've finished in the kitchen."

For the next few minutes Sam and Amanda worked side by side getting Caroline and Sara bathed and then ready for bed. From time to time their elbows would bump together, sending tiny shock waves of emotion through Amanda's body. Never in her wildest imaginings had she ever pictured herself in a perfect family setting as this one. She reveled in the moment, and yet, she knew it would be over soon.

"Okay, girls," Sam said. "It's time for bed."

Soon after Caroline and Sara were tucked in their beds for the night, Sam turned out the light in their room.

"Good night, girls," he said, standing in the

doorway. Amanda was right behind him, trying desperately to keep her emotional guards from collapsing. After hugging the girls good-night, her feelings were swelled up in her throat like a giant tidal wave.

"Good night, Daddy," they replied. "Good night, Amanda."

A piercing pain struck Amanda's heart. Just how much bittersweet joy was she supposed to handle in one, single night? The truth was, this should have been her life, period. Permanently. And it wasn't fair that it wasn't. "Good night, Caroline—Sara," she finally said, trying hard to keep her voice steady. The last thing she wanted was to alarm them by starting to cry. Besides, she was tougher than that—wasn't she? "Take care of your puppy. What's her name again?" she asked with a teasing smile.

"Sugar," they replied in unison.

"Then take care of Sugar."

"We will," they replied.

Sam shut their bedroom door, and immediately Amanda turned and marched down the hall toward the front door. Somehow she knew she had to get out of the house—fast—otherwise, she was going to get swallowed up in that tidal wave of hers.

"Wait a minute, Amanda. What about the coffee?" Sam said, following at her heels.

"It's getting too late for me to stay," she said,

making up any excuse she could while not missing a step on her way out. Suddenly, though, she felt as if she were running for her life. As if she had to get out of there, or else. And, indeed, it was the *or else* that had her moving toward the door like a roadrunner.

Just as she entered the living room, she stepped on something round—a toy, perhaps—that rolled forward a couple of inches and threw her off balance. She tripped over some other contraption on the floor, and before she knew what was happening, she was sprawled, belly-down, across the armrests of a big, brown leather recliner. Needless to say, the wind was knocked out of her. And her shoes... She had no idea where they were. One thing for sure, they weren't on her feet.

What a spectacle she must have made.

Amanda groaned. If only she had been watching where she was going, none of this would be happening to her. How embarrassing.

Quick as a shot, Sam was there, taking her gently by the shoulders and helping her to her feet. "Amanda," he exclaimed breathlessly, concern evident in his voice. "Are you all right?"

Amanda gave him a dazed look. "I—I'm fine," she stammered, trying to find her breath, her shoes and her sense of dignity, all at the same time.

"Hey, don't be in so big a rush to get up. You hit that recliner pretty hard."

"I know," she replied, still trying to catch her breath. Her knees were trembling. "Maybe I should sit down for a moment."

"Yeah," he said. "Maybe you should."

But instead of letting her just sit down on the recliner that was right there, he quickly scooped her up in his strong arms as if she were weightless—as he had Lucy—and carried her over to the sofa. "Lie here for a while," he said, carefully placing her down on the soft cushions.

"I don't need to lie down," Amanda argued, attempting to rise. The fact was, she still felt the need to run. And yet, she was still so rattled from her clumsy fall that she probably couldn't have made it two feet toward the door.

"Yes, you do," Sam insisted, holding her shoulders steady until she stopped struggling against him. She gave him a maddening frown that said she was the doctor here—not him—hoping that in some way it would make him realize just how frustrated she was with him, and herself, too. But if he understood, he didn't let on. Instead, he returned her frown, only in an amused sort of way.

"You're making too much of this," Amanda stated, after he finally let go of her shoulders. But she felt breathless—and scared silly that he might decide to touch her again. She was going to explode if he did.

"Maybe so," he said, once again looking concerned. "But I'd rather be safe than sorry."

"And I'd rather be on my way."

"That's obvious. But you're not going anywhere, Doc, until I'm positive that you're all right."

"I'm telling you, I'm okay," she said. Then she flung out her arms without really thinking of what she was implying for him to do. "See for yourself," she added.

Her heart was pounding.

He sat down on the edge of the sofa and began examining her arm.

"What do you think you're doing?" she asked, her eyes widening, her stomach tightening into knots.

"I'm taking you up on your offer. Let's see," he said, suddenly growing thoughtful. "Where exactly should I begin?"

"Begin what?"

"Begin to see if you're hurt."

"You are not a doctor," she said. "You're... you're..."

He was the sexiest man she had ever met. But that didn't give him the credentials to examine her.

Or did it?

Not hardly.

No way.

By now Amanda could barely breathe, much

less talk. There was an enormous pressure building in her—not to mention a suffocating heat rising to the surface of her skin. Her body was on fire. No doubt, if Sam were to decide to put those big, wide hands of his on any part of her body within the next few moments, she was going to suffer a major meltdown.

"Maybe I should start here," he said. He began to examine her shoulders and neckline, gently pressing his fingers into her skin. Eventually, his moves became a gentle massage. "Does this hurt?" he asked, pulling his eyebrows into a thoughtful frown.

"No," she replied immediately, wanting him to know that she didn't approve of his tactics. But nothing she ever said seemed to faze him from doing what he wanted. Besides, instead of sounding frustrated, she had sounded breathless.

Amanda glared at him. "If you were a real doctor and I were a real patient, this examination would get you into a lot of trouble," she said as a warning.

He grinned. "We both know I'm not a real doctor."

"And I'm not a real patient."

"Yeah," he said, amused. "So you've said."

"I want to get up," she stated, still glaring at him. She had to do something to keep herself from giving in to the wonderful sensations going through her body.

"In a minute, Amanda," he drawled. "Don't always be in so big a hurry."

And then the tips of his fingers pressed deeper into her skin and Amanda lost all track of what she wanted to say. Every pulse point in her body began a countdown to the moment when she would surely lose control.

She was in big trouble now. She needed to put a stop to this, she told herself.

And she wanted to, no doubt about it. But she didn't. Actually she couldn't. She didn't have the will in that moment to move a muscle, much less remove his hands from her body. She was mesmerized by the feel of his warm fingers on her skin.

She was hot, all right, and getting hotter by the second. And that, she knew, was no way for her to behave. Not if she wanted to keep her sanity.

"Sam..."

"Shh..." he said. "I'm almost done." He massaged his way down her arms. "Does any of this hurt?"

"No," she said softly.

"This?"

"No."

Finally, he applied a mild pressure along her collar bone. "How about here?" he asked.

"Uh-uh," she said, swallowing hard.

This examination was getting more and more difficult for her to handle. She felt flushed—hot.

She was definitely on overload. Something was bound to give at any moment.

Sam lifted his gaze and his eyes locked with hers. And within the next few moments she realized that something that should never happen between them was about to and she unconsciously moistened her lips. "Sam, I think this has gone far enough. Let me up before one of us does something we'll later regret."

As though he hadn't heard a word she had said, Sam cupped the sides of her face with his hands. "I'm going to kiss you, Amanda," he announced as he leaned into her face.

"No, you can't do that," she exclaimed. "This isn't supposed to be happening." But her voice was already so deep with desire that Amanda felt certain he could sense her need. As it was, his mouth was so close to hers that she could feel the warmth of his breath.

Pausing, he gazed into her eyes as though he were going to consume her at any moment. He began rubbing one of his thumbs back and forth across her bottom lip. Amanda heard her own intake of breath.

"I know you want me," he said huskily. But before she could even answer him, he caught her bottom lip between his teeth and passed the tip of his tongue across it.

It was the last straw. Amanda had no more control left. She did want him—bad.

Shame on her.

It was too late to worry about shame. Wrapping her arms around his neck, she knew she had passed that point a long time ago.

Sam groaned when her arms went around his neck and a moment later, he consumed her mouth—her total being—in a sweet, but urgently passionate kiss.

Amanda had never been kissed so completely, so thoroughly in her life. She found herself filled with an intense hunger. She wanted him. She had to have him. There was no other way to get the satisfaction she was now craving.

But how could she even consider taking this moment a step further?

No doubt about it, it was cooldown time. For both of them.

Sam pulled away before she did and gazed deeply into her eyes. He was breathing hard. Amanda was, too.

"We can't do this," Amanda said.

"I know. The kids," he replied.

"It's not just the kids. It's everything," she said. "I don't want to get involved with you—or anyone, for that matter."

"Yeah," he drawled a moment later. "I know what you mean. I feel the same way."

Now that hurt, especially after the way he had just kissed her.

Amanda sighed. "Please let me up. I need to go," she said.

"I know you do," he replied. "And I will—in a minute." Then he took her lips again, more gently this time, and Amanda didn't have the will-power to say no.

A sound coming from down the hall caught Amanda's attention. Sam heard it, too, because he suddenly stopped moving. Then they heard the faint sound again. This time, they recognized it as Sara's voice, calling for her father.

Sam stood up immediately. "I need to see about Sara. But I'll be right back."

"I'm leaving, Sam."

"No, don't," he said. "Not 'til I get back."

"I'm leaving now. It's pointless for me to stay."

Amanda saw when Sam clenched his teeth. He didn't say a word, but then he didn't have to for her to know he wasn't very happy with her.

Well, she wasn't all that happy with herself, either.

He turned and headed down the hall to check on Sara.

It took Amanda only a moment to rise from the sofa and gather up her things. She walked out, knowing that she was leaving a part of herself behind. But at least she had held herself together in front of him.

Because tonight had cost her plenty.

In fact, much more than she could have ever imagined.

It took Sam several minutes to assure Sara that there were no monsters under her bed where he had put her down for the night. He not only looked under it, but behind her curtains and inside her closet, as well. Then he sprayed those places with his antimonster solution—a homemade remedy of water and vanilla flavoring. It had worked for him when he was a kid, and now it worked for his girls. They usually slept like babies once he made their bedroom monster-free.

Once he finished, he walked back into the living room to find Amanda gone. Of course, she had said she wouldn't be there and he had no reason to believe otherwise. He had just hoped.

The truth was, he didn't know what he was doing. That was the effect she had on him. No other woman—not even his first wife—had made him this crazy.

"Dammit," he muttered under his breath.

Frustrated with her—with himself—he walked to the front window and glanced out. What was the woman trying to do to him, anyway? Drive him insane?

He'd had enough of this, he thought. He didn't need Amanda. He didn't need any woman. He just needed a little fun in his life. He was only human, after all.

In fact, he had heard someone in town mention that there was an all-night honky-tonk somewhere nearby, and as soon as Mrs. Cunningham was able, he was going to have her baby-sit for him so he could find it and have himself one hell of a good time. By golly, he deserved it.

And after he had that night out on the town, Dr. Amanda Lucas would be out of his system.

But until that night came, there was no use trying to fool himself. Sam knew he was going to think about her.

Often.

He damned sure was.

The following morning, Sam got up and cooked pancakes for his kids using the recipe Mrs. Cunningham had given him. They turned out okay. At least, the girls ate them. Afterward, he got them dressed for church. They arrived at the midmorning service just as it was starting.

When it was over, Caroline and Sara were in a hurry to get home to see about their puppy. But Sam needed to put gasoline in his truck and drove to the nearest service station. He felt as grouchy as a bear this morning, but he was doing his best not to let it show.

Not for one moment since he had awakened that morning had he been able to put Amanda from his mind.

He pulled up to a service pump and got out to fill his tank. Just then he saw Amanda coming out of the pay station. Looking around, he noticed her car was parked at the full-service island.

Suddenly, without any warning, he felt his temper rising.

"Amanda," he called out as he reached the rear of his truck. He saw her feet falter momentarily, but then she quickly picked up her pace. "Amanda, wait," he called out again, this time even louder than before.

Finally she halted and turned slowly around to face him. In five long strides he caught up with her.

"You're really good at running away, aren't you?" he said.

She widened her eyes. "I beg your pardon?"

"Come on, Amanda. We both know you ran away last night."

Amanda gaped at him. "For your information, I did not run away from you last night. I told you the reason I was leaving. It was pointless for me to stay."

"You could've waited the few minutes it took me with Sara."

"Of course, I could've waited," Amanda said, holding her head high. "But I didn't want to."

"Okay," Sam said, shaking his head. "I'll accept that. But I want to know one thing. What made you stay in the first place? I mean, I know the girls wanted you over for supper, but what made you decide to stay?"

"I like your children. A lot."

"Yeah, well, they like you, too." Sam stared at her for several long seconds. "Look," he finally said, "my kids don't need a bleeding heart. If that's what you're offering them, find someone else's kids to feel sorry for."

"I don't feel sorry for them—well, in a way, I do. And why shouldn't I? I know what they're going through. I lost my mom at a young age, too."

"I'm sorry, but you seem to think you have all the solutions where my girls are concerned."

"Of course not," Amanda replied.

"From now on, just stay away from my kids. They don't need your charity. Is that clear?"

"Perfectly," she replied, her voice cracking.

"Good," he said, turning on his heels and marching back to his truck. He couldn't recall ever being so fired up at someone other than the enemies he pursued as a navy SEABEE. Then again, he'd never had a woman get under his skin like Amanda Lucas.

"Women," he said with a shake of his head. "Who needs 'em?"

The only answer he got was an immediate tightening in his chest.

When he got to his truck, he glanced back and saw that Amanda was still standing in the spot where he'd left her. It looked as though her eyes were glistening with tears. But he couldn't be sure.

Climbing behind the wheel, he wondered if he'd done the right thing by telling Amanda to stay away from his girls. She clearly loved them, and he knew they were crazy about her.

Of course he'd been right, he told himself a moment later.

The problem was, could *he* stay away from her?

Chapter Seven

Amanda's encounter with Sam at the service station had turned her world upside down, and she couldn't wait to get home. After parking her car in the garage, she hurried inside and plopped her bag of groceries on the countertop.

He had accused her of running away from him.

How absurd. It was just like a man to put her down for something he didn't understand.

And now he didn't want her around his kids.

Never in a million years would she have done anything to hurt his kids. And, somehow, she knew he was aware of that fact. So, what was his real problem with her?

Undoubtedly, when she got into bed for the night, she was going to have herself a good cry.

Somehow she would find a way to prove herself to him. If for no other reason, than to satisfy herself.

Determined not to think of Sam for the time being, she took off her coat, hung it on a hook near the back door and then checked her answering machine. There weren't any messages from the hospital, but there was one from Lucy Foreman. Frowning in concern, Amanda dialed the number to the Foreman house.

Lucy answered and immediately launched into a conversation that included inviting Amanda to a small dinner party a week from Friday night. "This is something I've been planning to do since I had my baby at your office," Lucy said.

"That's not necessary," Amanda said.

"I know. But Tom's doing all the work. Say you'll come," Lucy said brightly.

"Well, I don't know...."

"Oh, please come," Lucy said.

Amanda frowned to herself. Now how, she wondered, could she refuse an invitation like that? Besides, Lucy was probably going to have the dinner party with or without her.

"I hope Mr. Arquette can attend," Lucy said. "I haven't called him yet."

"I see," Amanda replied.

"Is his coming a problem for you?" Lucy asked hesitantly.

"Problem? No, not at all," Amanda replied quickly. Almost too quickly. She took a deep breath to steady her nerves.

"Good. Then Tom and I will expect to see you on Friday evening, eight o'clock."

"Thank you, Lucy," Amanda said. "I'm looking forward to it." Frowning, she hung up the telephone and turned to head down the hall.

Suddenly, Amanda found herself thinking about the dinner party—about the fact that Sam might be in attendance—and she discovered that she was looking forward ever so slightly to the gathering. After all, in more ways than one, it might be the perfect opportunity to prove herself to Sam Arquette. In fact, she hadn't felt such a challenge in years. Of course, first, she had to get herself ready. She had to buy a new dress. And a new pair of shoes. She needed a haircut and she might even consider having her hairdresser add a few highlights to her hair. Time was going to be her biggest problem. Her work schedule was always so busy. But, somehow, she would get everything she needed done before the dinner party. It was that important to her.

It turned out Amanda was right about her schedule. The next couple of days were exceptionally busy for her and left her very little time to think about anything but work. She delivered two babies on Monday and one early Tuesday morning. Needless to say, she didn't have time for running personal errands.

Because it was later than usual when Amanda finally climbed into bed on Tuesday night, she immediately fell into a sound sleep.

At some point during the night—which turned out to be just past one o'clock in the morning—the telephone next to her bed rang at least five or six times before she stirred enough to reach for the receiver and bring it to her ear. "Hello," she said in a groggy voice.

"Amanda?"

"Yes." She still had her eyes closed.

"It's Sam."

Her eyes sprang open. "Sam?" She sat up in bed. "What's wrong?" She knew it had to be something. Why else would he be calling her at this time of night?

"It's Caroline," he said. "She has a fever."

"Did you call her doctor?"

"No. I called you."

"What's her temperature?"

"One hundred and one. And she says her throat hurts."

Amanda's heart picked up tempo. Caroline—sick? It felt as though someone was telling her her own child was ill. Throwing back the covers on her bed, she planted her feet on the floor. "From what I understand from my colleagues, there's a lot of strep going around, especially among younger children. You need to call her doctor.''

"Can't you examine her?" Sam asked.

"Well, yes, I can. But I'm not a pediatrician."

"I know. But Caroline wants you."

"She wants me?" Amanda repeated in awe, a warm feeling suddenly spreading throughout her body.

"She trusts you," Sam said.

A huge lump formed in Amanda's throat. Never before had someone asking for her as their physician meant so much to her.

"Look," Sam said, his tone of voice deepening. "I think she's scared. It's the first time she's been sick since she lost her mother. All I know is, she's asking for you."

That was it for Amanda. She had to get to Caroline's side as soon as possible. "I'll be there in ten minutes," she said, knowing that nothing short of a world catastrophe could keep her from going to the Arquette farm. For the first time in her career, this was going to be a very, very personal house call for her.

Hanging up the telephone, she got dressed, made sure her medical bag was in the trunk of her car and drove toward the Arquette farm.

The front porch light was on when she arrived. And before she could even knock on the door, Sam was opening it. "Hi," he said, his eyes meeting hers. "I'm glad you came."

"Where is she?" Amanda asked.

"In her bed. I put Sara in my bedroom so she could sleep."

Amanda nodded.

Somehow, without saying a word, they both knew they had a common goal now, and the protective barriers they usually held up against each other were lowered for the time being. This was one time they needed each other's support, and they both knew it.

Amanda hurried down the hall with Sam at her heels. But as she drew closer to Caroline's room, she began walking with more composure. Automatically switching into her doctor mode, she entered the child's bedroom, sat down on the edge of the mattress and placed her medical bag on the floor at her feet. Amanda knew that Sam was standing right behind her. She glanced back at him and saw he had placed his hands on his hips and was watching her every move. It was his parental instincts, she knew. Well, Caroline and Sara were special to her, too. But she couldn't think about her personal feelings right now. She had a job to do, and she couldn't let her emotions get in the way. It was enough that Sam was practically breathing down her neck.

Amanda placed her hand on Caroline's forehead

and the little girl opened her eyes. "Hi, precious," Amanda said, giving her a warm, caring smile. "Your daddy tells me that you aren't feeling very well."

Caroline shook her head. "Uh-huh."

"Is something hurting you?" Amanda asked.

"My throat," Caroline replied, and tears filled her eyes.

"Don't cry, dumpling," Sam said. "Everything's going to be okay. Amanda's here to help you get well."

Amanda smiled. "Your daddy's right. Everything is going to be okay. Now, can I have a look at your throat?"

"Will you make it all better?" the child asked.

"I'm going to try," Amanda replied, her heart going out to her. This wasn't just any child. This time was altogether different for Amanda.

Caroline nodded her approval.

Amanda smiled, then got the mini flashlight and a tongue depressor from inside her medical bag. "Open wide," she told Caroline, and the little girl obeyed her.

"Mmm..." Amanda said. "Her throat's spotted. She has an infection, all right."

"Strep?" Sam asked in concern.

"Possibly. But we won't know for sure until a throat culture is done."

"When?"

Amanda squeezed Caroline's hand and then glanced back at Sam. "If she were my child, I'd do it first thing tomorrow morning. If it's streptococcus, then she'll have to be given antibiotics. Is she allergic to any medications?"

"No—not that I know of." There was a hint of panic in Sam's voice.

Picking up on it, Amanda reached back and touched his arm. "Hey, don't look so worried. She'll be all right."

"I know," he replied. Then he lifted his eyes to hers. "I just hate seeing her sick."

"Have you given her something for the fever?"

"Yeah," Sam replied. "About a half hour ago."

"Good. I'm going to check it again now."

In no time at all, Amanda had a reading. "It's dropped eight-tenths of a degree," she said.

"That's a good sign, isn't it?" Sam asked, worry etched across his face.

"Yes," Amanda replied cheerfully, hoping to keep both the child and her father as calm as possible.

Smiling at Caroline, she said, "Honey, I want you to let me swab your throat with some medication I have with me. It won't hurt. And once it's done, the pain won't be as much, and you'll be able to fall back to sleep. And if it's okay with you," she added, taking Caroline's hand in hers,

"I'd like to stay right here at your side until you do."

For just a moment Caroline's eyes regained their sparkle and Amanda knew she had the child's approval for both swabbing her throat and for staying with her until she was asleep again.

Sam hovered even closer to see what she was doing as she medicated Caroline's throat. When she was done, he said, "I think I'll go make a pot of coffee. My nerves could stand a cup."

After sighing heavily from the tension, Amanda glanced back at him and said, "Mine, too."

He walked around to the other side of the bed, leaned down and kissed Caroline on the forehead. "I'll be right back, dumpling," he said to her.

Sam left the room and Amanda tucked Caroline's blanket in place around her. "Sleep tight, little one," she said, placing a featherlight kiss on Caroline's forehead in almost the same fashion as Sam. And then, as if it were something she did every night for her own children—which, of course, was a fantasy at best—Amanda began to hum a soft, sweet lullaby.

When Sam came back to his daughter's bedroom a few minutes later, the scene that confronted him stopped him cold in his tracks. He could only stare. For a moment, his whole system shut down. It was so poignant, so…natural to see Amanda at Caroline's bedside, humming a tune. But, of course, he certainly didn't want to pursue that train of thought. Amanda was a great doctor, and he was going to leave it at that.

"Is she asleep?" he whispered, finally walking into the room.

"I think so," Amanda replied, rubbing the back of her neck.

Sam knew Amanda was tired. She had to be. She worked practically twenty-four hours a day. Where, he wondered, did she get her stamina? Without even thinking of what he was doing, he walked up behind her and placed his hands on her shoulders. Moving his thumbs in small, circular movements, he began working out the tenseness in her muscles.

"Thanks for coming here like this in the middle of the night," he said, now searching to find a valid excuse for what he was doing. "I know you must be tired. I really do appreciate it."

Amanda's breath locked in her throat. His hands had begun to work magic on her tired muscles. And, heaven help her, it felt so good, she didn't want him to stop. This time, instead of listening to the warning bells going off in her head, she listened to her heart. Closing her eyes, she moaned. "Mmm…you're pretty good at this," she murmured.

Realizing what she had just said, Amanda sat up straight and cleared her throat. A moment later, clutching her medical bag in her hand, she rose to her feet. "The only thing you can do for now is keep an eye on her fever. If it should spike, bring her to the emergency room. But I doubt if that will happen," she added rather quickly. "In the morning, take her to her pediatrician for a throat culture. I'm almost certain she is going to need medication." She paused, waiting for Sam to speak. When he didn't, she said, "Do you have any questions?"

"Ah, none that I can think of right now. Aren't you staying?"

"Staying?" Amanda said in confusion.

"For the rest of the night. What if Caroline wakes up again?"

"I think she'll sleep the rest of the night."

"Look, I have a spare bedroom, and there's always the sofa."

Amanda paused, unable to believe what he was saying. Did he actually think she would stay for the rest of the night?

"Sam, there's no need for me to stay. Caroline is going to be just fine."

With one last lingering look at both father and daughter, Amanda headed for the door.

Sam was following right on her heels as she entered the living room. "You're running away again, aren't you?"

"That's ridiculous. I might make house calls, but I don't spend the night."

"We're not talking about house calls and you know it. I'm talking about *you* not wanting to stay here with *me*."

"That's your opinion and you have a right to it. I happen to have my own opinion."

"And what is that?"

"I'm simply protecting myself."

"From what?"

"Involvement," she answered without stopping to glance back at him.

Suddenly, Sam took two long strides and was standing in front of her, blocking her path to the front door.

"I'm not asking you to get involved," he said, placing his hands on his hips. "Frankly, I'm not interested in an involvement, either."

Amanda frowned. "Then what do you want from me?"

This time it was Sam who frowned. Shaking his head, he said, "To tell you the truth, I don't know. But what I do know is that tonight Caroline needed a doctor, so I called you."

"And I came," Amanda replied.

"Yeah," he said, then glanced down at the floor momentarily before bringing his gaze up to level with hers. "I'm not being completely truthful with you. I guess somewhere in the back of my mind, I was thinking that the two of us could get involved."

"Oh, really," Amanda said, a lump swelling in her throat. "Tell me, Sam, are you looking to have a fling with me?"

"Not a fling, exactly."

"What then? A full-fledged, long-term affair?"

"Hell, I don't know," Sam said, running his fingers through his hair.

"Is that how you think of me? As a potential mistress?" she asked, her eyes brimming with tears.

"No, of course not," he replied.

"Then what? As a wife?"

"It's too soon to think about marriage at all right now—not even to you."

"Really?" she replied heatedly. "Well, let me give you a little advice before you ever decide to think in those terms about me. I'm barren. Do you know what that means? It means I can't have children of my own."

"I know what it means," Sam replied, only his voice was no longer harsh. He took a step toward her. "Amanda, I—I don't know what to say. I'm so sorry."

"Well, like you once told me about your girls, I don't need your pity. I have a fulfilling career and a good reputation in the area. I'm doing just fine."

"Yeah, I can see that," he said in a way that let her know he didn't believe one word of it. "Come here,'' he said, pulling her into his arms. He held her close.

It was heaven to have his big, strong arms as her sanctuary, even if it was only temporary. She wrapped her arms around his waist and held on.

"Look at me, Amanda," he whispered.

There was no use denying it. Her willpower was shattered. She did as he bid.

And then he took her lips in a soft, sweet kiss that warmed her insides to the tips of her toes. When the kiss finally ended, he didn't pull away, but placed his forehead against hers.

Amanda was dangerously close to falling apart. If she was going to save even a shred of her pride, she knew what she had to do.

Moistening her lips, she said, "I've got to go."

"No, you don't," Sam said. "You could stay."

"No. Please, let me go."

For what seemed a timeless moment, he pulled away just enough to gaze deeply into her eyes. "Are you sure this is how you want it?"

Holding her emotions tightly in check, Amanda gave a slight nod.

"Can I call you tomorrow?"

"No," she replied. Then, lifting her medical bag from the floor where she'd dropped it, she added, "We both know it would never work."

Without further resistance from him, she turned and walked out the door.

* * *

Sam didn't sleep at all that night and was up bright and early the next morning. One of the first things he did was call and make Caroline an appointment at the doctor's office. By midmorning they were in the physician's office. The pediatrician diagnosed Caroline with a mild case of strep throat and gave her a prescription for penicillin, which Sam had filled at the nearest pharmacy. Then he drove home and made sure that Caroline went straight to bed. Without her sister to play with, Sara kept herself entertained with their new puppy.

The first moment Sam got to himself, he sat down with a cup of coffee. And, of course, all too soon, his thoughts turned to the one person whom he wished he didn't think about so often. Amanda.

What she had told him last night hadn't completely registered until after she was gone. Only then had the weight of her words sunk in. She couldn't have children. How tragic for someone who obviously loved them. Who devoted her life to bringing them into the world. What he didn't understand was why she held that world—men, in particular—at a distance.

She was an enigma, all right. An enigma he couldn't figure out and couldn't stop thinking about. But he knew one thing for sure. Underneath her iceberg facade was a flesh-and-blood woman he wanted to make love with.

Sam rose from the kitchen chair where he had been sitting and checked the pantry, only to find he was in short supply of canned soups and juices, the very foods Caroline needed while she was convalescing. He called Mrs. Cunningham to see if she would be able to stay with the girls while he went back into town for groceries.

Within the hour Sam found himself standing in the middle of a grocery aisle, examining the labels on canned goods. Finally, he had what he came for, checked out at the register and started for home.

Suddenly, he got a wild idea. Since it was close to noon, maybe Amanda would consider having lunch with him. It was going to be a long week ahead with Caroline sick and all. Besides, he had told Amanda he would call her with news about Caroline. He would just give it to her in person instead.

He drove straight to her office.

"Hi," the young receptionist said when she saw him.

Sam cleared his throat. "Would you please tell Amanda that I'm here to see her," he said.

The young woman widened her eyes. "D-did you say *Amanda?*"

"That's right," Sam said, perplexed. "She is in, isn't she?"

"W-well, yes, but—never mind," she said as though she remembered this scenario from their past conversation and now knew the drill. "I'll get her."

Sam nodded in reply.

A short time later, Amanda entered the reception area.

"Sam, what are you doing here?"

For a moment, Sam wondered the same thing himself.

It was obvious that she was still seeing patients—and none too happy to see him.

He probably looked like a complete fool.

Who was he kidding? He was a fool.

"Would you like to have lunch with me?" he asked.

Amanda frowned. "Sam, you know I can't."

"Too busy?"

"Well, yes," she said hesitantly, pulling him aside to where their conversation couldn't be easily overheard. "But that's not the only reason, and you know it." She leaned forward and spoke in a lowered voice. "We discussed this last night."

"No, *you* discussed this last night. I barely got a word in edgewise."

"How's Caroline?" she asked. "I was planning to call as soon as I got a break from seeing patients."

"You were right," Sam said, knowing she was

deliberately changing the subject. "She has strep throat. The doctor gave her a prescription for some oral antibiotics."

"Give her plenty of liquids."

"Yeah, I know. Mrs. Cunningham has already given me those instructions."

"Well, then," Amanda said, taking in a deep breath. "I'd better get back to my patients. You will see yourself out, won't you?"

"Amanda," Sam began. "We can't just never talk about last night again."

"I don't see why not," she replied.

"Because nothing was settled."

"For me, it was." She turned to go.

"Wait," Sam said, touching her elbow. "I didn't really get to think about what you told me until after you were gone."

"Good. It was probably for the best that way."

"There's so much I don't understand," he argued.

Amanda whirled around. "Look, Sam. If ever you decided to remarry again, wouldn't you want more children?"

"Well, yes, I suppose so," he replied.

"I think I've made my point," she said.

"Now just a minute, Amanda."

"No. Please, leave me alone."

Sam took a step back. "Fine. I will."

"Good," Amanda replied, pivoting on her heels and marching away.

A moment later, Sam exited her office with a vow to forget about her. She was too complicated. He didn't have time for that kind of trouble.

He had his head convinced. Now if he could just convince his heart.

Amanda was so shaken by the encounter with Sam that she had to go into the privacy of her office to regroup before going on to examine her next patient. Closing her eyes, she breathed deeply. She had a right to try to keep her heart in one piece, didn't she?

And yet, somehow, she already knew that it was too late for that.

She was over the line.

Her heart was already in a million pieces because of him.

The next day, Amanda tried to keep herself busy so that she wouldn't think about Sam—or his children. But that night before going to bed, she gave in to her inner struggle and called him. After all, she had the perfect excuse. She could always say she was calling to check on how the girls were doing—Caroline, in particular.

Which was the truth, of course. Only, it wasn't

the whole truth. She wanted to hear Sam's voice, too. She just didn't want to have to tell him that.

Sam answered the telephone on the third ring and immediately Amanda's heart went into a wild galloping beat.

"Sam, it's Amanda," she said. She held her breath momentarily.

There was a brief pause on the other end of the line. In that one single second Amanda's heart went from a galloping beat to a sudden stop. She imagined all sorts of things going through his head. But, finally, he said, "Hi."

Amanda took a deep breath. "I hope you weren't asleep," she said.

Sam cleared his throat. "No."

Amanda swallowed down the sudden lump in her throat. "I—I thought I'd call to check on the girls," she stammered. "How's Caroline doing? And Sara? I hope Sara hasn't come down with what Caroline has."

"As a matter of fact," he said rather stiffly, "Caroline is doing much better. And, no, Sara didn't get sick." He cleared his throat again. "Uh, look, Amanda, I've got company right now. Can I call you back later?"

Amanda's heart sank. He had company?

"I—I'm sorry," Amanda stammered. "I didn't mean to disturb you."

"Look, I promise to call you back," Sam said.

"You don't have to. It really isn't necessary," she said, trying to recover her equilibrium.

"Amanda—"

"Good night, Sam," she said, hanging up the telephone. For some reason she felt sick to her stomach.

By the time she had taken a shower and turned down her bed for the night, Amanda was ready to have herself a good, long cry.

Chapter Eight

It was Friday, and as always Amanda's workday was hectic. But at least she wasn't on call this weekend. She was going to have plenty of time to curl up in bed and feel sorry for herself.

During the morning Lucy Foreman called her office and left a message reminding Amanda about the dinner party that night, and Amanda realized that somehow—because of her emotional state, she supposed—she had forgotten all about it. Sam was definitely going to be there. Sam and perhaps his overnight guest would be accompanying him. Uh-uh. No way. She wasn't a glutton for punishment.

"What are you wearing, Doc?" Kathy asked after handing her the message.

"Huh? What? Oh, the dinner party. I'm not going," she replied.

Kathy's mouth dropped open. "Why not, for heaven's sake?"

"I can't. I'm busy."

"Doing what?" Kathy asked in disbelief.

Amanda realized that she would just as soon give Kathy an excuse so the woman would leave her alone. She didn't want to tell her it was because she didn't want to see Sam. She simply wasn't strong enough to handle being in his company. She needed more time.

As it was, all she could think about was him and that certain someone—a woman, she truly believed—whom he'd invited over to his house last night. It was killing her to even think of him being with another woman. In fact, it was eating her alive. Besides, he hadn't called her back.

"I've been too busy to go out and buy something to wear," she heard herself say finally.

"Well, that's not a problem," Kathy said, her eyes glittering. "I think we're about the same size, and I happen to have a closet full of dresses you can wear. Some I haven't even worn. In fact, I know of one in particular that would look great on you. It's black and low-cut down the back—and s-e-x-y."

"I'm not into sexy, Kathy," Amanda replied blandly. "You know that's not me."

"Well, it could be, if you wanted it to. Be daring, Doc."

Daring?

Didn't Kathy realize whom she was talking to?

Daring for her was driving home from the hospital late at night a couple of miles per hour over the speed limit. She liked playing it safe. And she had been safe, until Sam Arquette stormed into her life.

But for her to go to a party wearing a black, sexy-looking dress when she knew he would be there was simply too much.

Wasn't it?

Suddenly, Amanda found herself hesitating with her answer. It had been a long time since she had wanted to let herself feel sexy.

What would Sam think of her if she did wear Kathy's black dress to the dinner party tonight? Would he even notice? She began to have second thoughts about the whole thing. "I don't know about this, Kathy," Amanda said, shaking her head.

Kathy placed her arm around her boss's shoulders. "Leave everything to me, Doc. I have all the accessories you can possibly need. If you want me to, I can even do your hair, nails and makeup. But I really think you should go to that dinner party."

"Yes, you're right," Amanda said, forcing herself to be daring for once in a long, long time. "I should go."

And now that she had made the decision, all she needed was Kathy's enthusiasm.

Oh, yeah, and that sexy dress of hers.

Sam glanced at the clock on the wall in his bedroom. Soon he would be leaving for the Foremans' dinner party. Already Mrs. Cunningham had arrived to baby-sit his girls. And yet, here he was still waiting on Amanda to return the message he'd left for her on her answering machine at home. He knew her well enough to know that it would be just like her to get home and ignore the blinking light altogether.

Damn the woman. She was driving him plum crazy. Besides his girls, she was all he ever thought about.

Frustrated, he grabbed hold of his telephone and dialed the number to Amanda's house. It rang until her answering machine picked up again. Refusing to leave another message, he hung up. A few moments later he slipped on his dinner jacket, walked out of his bedroom, then said goodbye to his two young daughters and their baby-sitter.

It was a cold night and Sam was glad when he arrived at the Foreman ranch. Tom Foreman answered the door, and since it was his and Sam's first time to meet, Tom had immediately introduced himself as Lucy's husband. Lucy was sitting on the sofa, holding their baby. Sam walked over to look at their infant son.

"Want to hold him?" Lucy asked.

Although Sam was taken off guard, he thought it was a great idea. He hadn't held a baby in a long time. The last one had been Sara, he thought, and already she was four years old. He immediately took the sleeping infant from Lucy's arms. "Hi, little fellow," he said. "Remember me?"

Just then the doorbell rang and Tom hurried to answer it. In less than a minute he reentered the living room with Amanda.

She looked sensational. She had on a sleek, off-the-shoulders, long-sleeved black dress. No doubt about it, she was a complete knockout. So much so, Sam couldn't take his eyes off her. In fact, he could hardly breathe.

He couldn't believe what he was seeing.

Her hair had been pinned up and she wore a pair of sparkling earrings that flirted with the dim lighting in the room. The cut of the dress made the line of her neck look long and lean, and he knew exactly where he wanted to place a kiss.

"Doc Lucas, I believe you know our other guest," Tom said.

"Yes, of course. Sam," she said, nodding her head in greeting.

All at once her gaze settled on the small bundle he had in his arms, and for a fraction of a second, her features softened. Using the rare moment to his advantage, Sam stepped forward with the infant. "Remember this little guy?" he said. "He was squalling the last time we saw him."

Amanda gazed down at the sleeping child, and Sam thought he noticed her eyes moistening—and now he knew why. Or, at least, he thought he did. She wanted her own baby—something, according to her, she could never have.

"Can I hold him?" she asked, quickly recovering.

"Sure," both Sam and Lucy said at the same time. Sam turned and Amanda took the baby from his arms.

The four adults conversed for a while with Tom telling Amanda and Sam how grateful he and Lucy were to them for helping deliver their son safely into the world. Eventually Lucy took her son to his nursery and put him down to sleep.

By the time she returned, dinner was ready to be served and all four adults moved to the dining room. As they were heading in that direction, Sam leaned close to Amanda's ear and said, "I want to talk to you in private."

"Please, Sam, there's nothing more to say."

"Well, I have plenty to say to you," he replied. "I'm following you home tonight, so we can talk."

"No."

"Yes."

"Sam..."

"I mean it, Amanda. I'm following you home and that's that."

She glared at him before taking the seat that Tom offered her.

Finally, they were all seated and enjoying their meal. Afterward, they had coffee and dessert. But by now the only thing Amanda could think about was the fact that Sam was going to be following her home as soon as the dinner party was over.

And, unfortunately, that was happening all too soon.

She and Sam said their goodbyes to the Foremans at the front door. Tom offered to walk Amanda to her car, but Sam intervened and said he would do the honor.

"Where're your keys?" he said to Amanda the moment they were out of earshot. She handed them to Sam and they walked side by side until they reached her car.

Once she was inside, he handed her her keys and said, "I'll see you at your house."

Without bothering to answer him, Amanda cranked her car's engine; put its automatic transmission in forward gear and drove off.

Fifteen minutes later she was parking her car in the garage when Sam pulled up behind her in the driveway. Soon they were entering her house.

Right away Amanda slipped off her coat and tossed it over the back of a chair. Then, taking a deep breath, she crossed her arms over her chest. Instead of feeling strong and in control, her heart was pounding just being near him.

"Okay," she said. "We both know that you've got something on your mind. So let's hear it."

Sam shook his head in what looked to be complete frustration. "How can I talk some sense into you when you're keyed up like this? For once in your life, Amanda, relax."

"I am relaxed," she replied stiffly.

Sam frowned. "You're practically standing at attention."

"Well, for your information, I don't happen to like being put on the spot the way I was at the Foremans'. What I can't figure out is why I let you get away with it."

Sam shrugged. "Probably because you had no choice."

"Exactly," she replied heatedly.

"Amanda," he said, "I'm in love with you. Doesn't that mean anything to you?" His eyes were intense…piercing…earnest.

"Don't say that," she replied, her eyes filling with tears, her heart pounding uncontrollably.

"Why not? It's true."

But for how long? Amanda wondered. A month? Two months? A year? Then he would begin to wonder what he was doing with a woman who couldn't give him more children. She knew the routine. And she wasn't about to fall for it.

Still, there was a part of her that wanted to take him at his word.

"Don't you see," he continued. "We're perfect for each other. We can make a life together. You can continue to have your career, and I can continue to take care of the children and the farm. Can't you see, I'm offering you a chance to have your career and a family, too. And whether or not you admit it, I think you want those things. You're just too hardheaded to admit it."

By now Amanda's pain was so deep and so raw that she thought surely she wasn't going to survive the next moment. Whirling around, she walked several feet away from him. Drawing in a long, steadying breath, she prayed for the courage she knew she would need to help get her through the following seconds.

"This isn't about my being hardheaded. It's about…I'm not perfect. I can't give you more children," she said almost angrily.

"I know that, and I've given it a lot of thought," he said. "We could always adopt, if we want."

"And what? Have you wake up one morning down the road and decide that you're tired of living with only half a woman? No, thank you. I can do without that."

"Is that what you think of me?" he asked, gaping at her.

"I'm just being realistic," she said.

"You're not even willing to give me a chance? Why not?"

"Look, I was engaged to be married once, to someone who also claimed to love me. But within a few hours of learning that I was infertile, my so-called fiancé no longer wanted me for his wife."

"I—I'm sorry about that," Sam said.

"Pity is exactly what I don't want from you."

"I don't pity you. I love you. Can't you understand that?"

Biting back her tears, Amanda turned away from him. "I just can't take the chance of going through something like that again. I just can't."

"Amanda, I'm only human, and I can't take much more of this, either. You know, don't you, that if I leave here like this tonight, I won't be coming back—ever."

Amanda swallowed back the lump in her throat. "Yes, I know," she finally said.

"Fine then," he replied, as if he were truly heartbroken. Moments later Amanda heard the door slam behind him.

All alone now, she crumpled into the nearest chair and sobbed her heart out.

Chapter Nine

The following morning Amanda woke to find her eyes all swollen and red from crying herself to sleep the night before. Not only that, but she had a throbbing headache. Struggling out of bed, she went to the kitchen, took two aspirin and made an ice pack for the pain in her head. Then she crawled back into bed and pulled the covers up to her neck. She was in no hurry to get up and face the day. She had wanted Sam out of her life. Well, now he was. And while she knew it was for the best, she was completely heartbroken.

Without a doubt, this was one heartache that was going to take her a lifetime to recover from.

In spite of everything that was going wrong in his life these days, Sam was trying his best to keep his spirits up. He fixed his girls breakfast and they all sat down to eat together. But he kept looking at the one empty chair opposite him, thinking that Amanda should have been sitting in it. She belonged with them. He knew that now. Heaven help him, but it wasn't as though he had been looking for someone to love. It had just happened.

He was tough, he told himself. He could take the blow. If Amanda didn't want to listen to reason, he couldn't make her. In fact, he was already getting himself started down the road to recovery. Tonight Mrs. Cunningham was going to baby-sit for him and he was going to find himself the smokiest, loudest honky-tonk around these parts. If Amanda was willing to settle for just a career, then why should he care? At least he had learned something about himself in all of this. He wasn't immune to falling in love.

Sam was ready that night when Mrs. Cunningham arrived at his house. He hugged his girls good-night while telling them to behave while he was gone. The last thing he heard as he was walking out the door was Mrs. Cunningham saying, "You had better not get yourself into trouble."

Someone from Mason's Grove had told him about a honky-tonk in the next county that had plenty of cold beer and enough good-looking women and loud country music to soothe any man's soul. He wheeled his truck in that direction and settled back in his seat with his radio set to a country music station. And although his heart was heavy with thoughts of Amanda, he had convinced himself that once he arrived at his destination, he was going to have himself one heck of a good time.

In fact, he was determined to.

And as it turned out, he did. Until around midnight. By then he'd had all he wanted of cold beer and loud, loud music. He had a headache and found himself sitting at a far corner of the bar next to a great-looking young woman...sobbing in his beer over Amanda.

What a bummer. The young woman looked absolutely bored stiff with him and, in truth, he didn't blame her.

His night out on the town really wasn't doing him any good. He was still mooning over Amanda. In his heart he knew that she was the only woman he really wanted to be with and no amount of beer or pretty women was going to change that.

"This is ridiculous," he said, suddenly throwing enough money on the bar to pay for his tab and then some. "I'm going home." He rose from his stool, turned and headed for the door.

There was a woman sitting at a table with two men. She saw him heading out and yelled, "Hey, good-lookin', where're ya goin'?"

"Home," he answered, looking her square in the face. "To the woman I love."

"Well, whoop-de-do," she replied, and then went back to her own business.

Sam left the bar.

He knew one thing. It wasn't going to be easy to convince Amanda of his feelings for her. She had a stone wall around her emotions three feet thick and ten feet high. But somehow he would get through it. He simply had to.

It was well into the night, but Amanda was still curled up in her bathrobe on one end of her sofa watching yet another tearjerker on late night television. It was her punishment for not having the courage to acknowledge her feelings for Sam. One of her all-time favorite movies, *The Way We Were,* was about to come on. She had her box of tissues right next to her and was ready for a good cry. By golly, she deserved one.

Suddenly, her doorbell rang. A moment later, before she could even rise from the sofa, she heard a man yell out, "Amanda, open up. It's me— Sam." Then he hit her doorbell again. Of course, she knew it was Sam. She would recognize his voice anywhere.

But then, her next thought was that something was wrong. Why else would he come banging on her door at this hour? With pulse racing to an all-time high, she was off the sofa in nothing flat. With only seconds passing, she had the door opened.

"What? What's wrong?" she asked, standing face-to-face with him. Then she got the faintest whiff of alcohol on his breath. She gaped at him. "Have you been drinking?"

"I had a couple beers," he said.

"What do you want?" she asked anxiously. "Are the girls all right?"

"Yeah, they're fine. They're with Mrs. Cunningham right now."

"Oh, thank goodness," she breathed.

Sam stepped inside her house and closed her door. "I need to talk to you, Amanda. Right now."

"At one o'clock in the morning?" she said. "I don't think so."

"Well, I do," he stated forcefully. "You happen to be the woman I love and want to marry. Therefore, I have my rights."

Amanda's heart felt heavy in her chest. "Sam, please, don't start that again. Not tonight." By now, her insides were in complete shambles.

Sam walked up to her, lifted her hand and placed it against his forehead. "Can you feel that I have a fever, Doc? Well, I do. I have one for you. And it's burning me up inside."

He brought her hand down and placed it over his heart. "Do you hear that?" he asked. "It's beating for you."

"Sam, you don't know what you're saying."

He placed his hand under her chin and lifted her head until she was looking directly into his eyes. "Tell me you don't feel the same about me."

"That's not the point, and you know it," she said, her voice trembling.

"It is the point, and it's the only point that matters. Sooner or later, Amanda, you're going to have to trust someone to love you. All I'm asking is for you to let that person be me. Me and my girls."

Amanda began shaking her head. "It's not that simple for me."

"But it is that simple. Can't you see how crazy in love I am with you? I left here the other night saying I would never return. And yet here I am. And I will always be here for you, Amanda."

"You say that," she replied. "But how do I know that it's true?"

"You've got to trust me, Amanda. There's no other way."

"But what if you decide at some point in your life that you would like to have more children? I won't be able to give them to you."

"We'll adopt. There are plenty of kids out there who need good, loving homes. I know you have your career, but since I'm retired from the navy, I like being home with the kids. Who knows what the future will bring? Sure, there'll be plenty of disappointments. That's life. But we'll have each

other to help us get through them. But you've got
to give us a chance first.''

It was all so sudden. Amanda wanted to believe
him. She really did.

Actually, she did believe him, and maybe that
was what was scaring her the most. Tears gathered
in her eyes.

Sam pulled her into his arms. "You want to trust
me, don't you?"

"I do trust you. Otherwise I would've never told
you what I did the other night," she said.

"Oh, Amanda, you're really something else,"
he said, gazing deep into her eyes. "No matter
what I do, I can't seem to stop thinking about
you."

"I can't stop thinking about you, either."

"It's crazy, isn't it, the way it happened just like
that?"

Amanda gave him a tentative smile. "It was sort
of mind-boggling, all right."

Suddenly, growing serious, Sam cupped the
sides of her face. "Amanda, I want you to marry
me and be a mother to my two children. Will
you?"

She was speechless. Finally, she whispered, "I
don't know what to say."

"Say yes, dammit," Sam replied, laughing.

Amanda took a deep, steadying breath. As a
doctor—as a human being—she knew this was a

give-and-take world. Fate had deemed it necessary to take away something very precious from her, her ability to have children of her own. Only now Fate was giving her something back in return. Something very, very precious. It was giving her Sam and his two little girls to love. All she needed was the courage to reach out and embrace the gift.

Amanda braced herself and then slipped her hands over his. "It would be the dream of my life to marry you."

Sam brought her face forward and kissed her thoroughly—passionately—on the lips. Then, pulling away, he said, "Let's get married now—as soon as possible. I want us together as a family on Thanksgiving Day. You, me and the girls. I love you, Doc, more than you'll ever know. I want you home with us where you belong."

"I love you, too," Amanda replied. "And, yes, let's get married right away."

Sam pulled Amanda back into his arms and kissed her longingly.

"By the way," he said. "Did I happen to mention to you that Josie Wentworth came by my place the other night? She and her family have put out an APB on Sabrina Jensen. I heard from her yesterday and they've already gotten a possible lead down in Wallace Canyon. The sheriff, Riley Hunter, is going to check it out for them."

"That's great news," Amanda said. "I'm so glad to hear that someone's finally seen her."

"Well, it's not for certain yet. We'll keep our fingers crossed, but it sure does sound hopeful."

"You know what?" Amanda said, her eyes shining with tears as she cupped the sides of his face. "How easy it is for me to see now that you're the one I've been waiting for all my life. You make me feel whole again. I love you."

Sam grinned. "I love you, too. Come on, let's sit on the sofa and smooch like I've been wanting to do with you since the moment I saw you."

"That's ridiculous. You didn't feel that way the moment you met me."

"Well, I darn sure did. The moment you opened your mouth, I fell madly in love with your voice."

"My voice?" Amanda said, laughing. Then she hurried to the sofa, motioning for him to follow.

He did.

"We can make plans later," she said. "Let's smooch first."

For all it was worth—and for Amanda, it was worth the world—Sam sealed their future with a kiss.

Epilogue

Three days later Amanda and Sam were married by a Justice of the Peace in the presence of Caroline, Sara, Mrs. Cunningham and Tom Foreman. They took a brief honeymoon to the mountains and returned home two days before Thanksgiving.

On the day set aside for giving thanks, Amanda and her new family gathered around the dinner table to count their many blessings.

"Daddy, can I have dessert first?" Sara asked. She was wearing the dress Amanda had given her for her birthday. Caroline was wearing a new dress, too. She wanted her girls to look their best.

"No, pumpkin. You have to eat your meal, then you can have dessert," Sam said. Wearing a pair of navy dress slacks, a white shirt and tie, he began carving the turkey Amanda had prepared.

"Can Sugar have some turkey, too?" Caroline asked.

"Of course," Sam replied, halting his task just long enough to look at Amanda and wink. "He's part of the family, too."

Amanda smiled. She felt like the luckiest woman alive.

After all, she had everything she could ever want.

She had Sam's love. And his girls to keep her busy. At last, her lifelong dream was complete. She was a wife and a mother. It was the most precious gift Sam could have given her. And she felt like a whole woman again.

And, in turn, she planned to cherish her husband, her children, always.

* * * * *

FOLLOW THAT BABY...

Join the search—a pregnant woman is missing when our fabulous new cross-line series continues with:

THE SHERIFF AND THE IMPOSTOR BRIDE
by Elizabeth Bevarly
in Silhouette Desire® next month!

And in future months look out for:

THE MILLIONAIRE AND THE PREGNANT PAUPER
by Christie Ridgway
January 2000, Desire™

THE MERCENARY AND THE NEW MUM
by Merline Lovelace
February 2000, Sensation™

The Sheriff and the Impostor Bride

Elizabeth Bevarly

Rachel Jensen tossed a limp, wayward length of tinsel back on the little plastic Christmas tree that squatted in her twin sister's rented picture window, and sighed with melodramatic melancholy. The single strand of variegated lights wound around the tree and flickered to an irregular rhythm, off and on, off…and…on, off and on, their flamboyant, if meager, celebration of color reflected on the window behind.

The view on the other side of the glass, however, was anything but merry and colorful. To the left, the flat, brown Oklahoma landscape stretched into oblivion beneath a slate sky—not a hill or dale or tree in sight. Every few seconds a snowflake interrupted the monotony, swirling up and around, dancing in the gusty wind that buffeted the rented mobile home.

Had she not already known already, Rachel would have guessed that the mobile home to which her twin had summoned her was a rental, because it was furnished in traditional rental style—ugly. Brown furniture, brown paneling, brown carpeting, brown cabinetry...with a little tan and beige thrown in here and there for good measure. Rachel swore that if she ever got out of Wallace Canyon— and, by golly, she *would* get out of Wallace Canyon the moment she located Sabrina—she would never buy anything brown again.

But until that time came, it looked as though she was going to have to settle for lots of it. And that time wouldn't come until she figured out just where in the heck Sabrina was, how in the heck her sister had gotten herself into such trouble, and what in the heck they were going to do to get her out of it again.

Because being in trouble just wasn't Sabrina's style at all. Sabrina was the levelheaded one of the twin sisters, the one who knew exactly what she wanted and exactly how to go about getting it. Rachel was the one more likely to find herself *in* things. In dire straits, for example. Or in deep doo-doo. Or in hock. Or in over her head.

Two nights ago, Sabrina had called Rachel at her job in a bustling, rough-and-tumble Oklahoma

City nightspot from this very mobile home. But Eddie, the bar manager, had caught Rachel behind the bar in the middle of the conversation—and at the height of the after-work Happy Hour crush. Before Rachel had had a chance to find out the particulars of Sabrina's situation, he'd jabbed his thumb down on the button to cut the connection short. There had only been time for Sabrina to make Rachel promise to come to Wallace Canyon, to the Westport Mobile Home Community, where she was renting the mobile home on lot thirty-two, as soon as possible.

But when Rachel had arrived at the appointed address yesterday afternoon—losing her job in Oklahoma City in the process, because she'd been scheduled to work yesterday—Sabrina had been nowhere in sight.

The mobile home's front door had been unlocked, though, and nothing inside seemed to have been disturbed. There was evidence of very recent habitation, but there were no clothes in the drawers or closets, nothing to indicate that Sabrina had been the one living here. Upon checking with the manager of the mobile home community, Rachel had learned that her twin sister had paid her rent through the end of the year—in cash. But Sabrina herself was nowhere to be found.

At this point, Rachel didn't know whether to stay or go. She didn't know if Sabrina was hiding out nearby, was making her way back home to Tulsa, or had left Oklahoma entirely. All Rachel *was* certain about was pretty much what she'd been certain about in the beginning, a few months ago, back when Sabrina had first taken off. Squat. She was certain about squat. Except for the fact that her sister was in trouble. And alone. And on the run. And unwilling to tell anyone the particulars of her situation.

Oh, yeah, And she was pregnant, too.

Pregnant. Now that was another completely un-Sabrina-like thing for Sabrina to have done. In the Most Likely to Be Knocked Up and Abandoned category, Rachel would have won hands down. Not that she slept around or anything like that. But she sure did tend to fall in love—and right back out again—way more than the average woman did.

Just like her mother, she thought before she could stop herself. Just like Blanche Jensen had done.

As quickly as the realization came to her, Rachel tried to think of something else. Instead, she reminded herself that it was Sabrina, not herself, who was single and in a family way. Sabrina, not herself, who was on the run from some shady threat. It was Sabrina who'd landed in trouble this time. Now if Rachel could figure out where her sister was, then maybe, just maybe, the two of them could put their identical heads together and come up with a solution.

For long moments, she pondered her dilemma, until a brisk rap at the front door roused her from her thoughts.

Rachel's head snapped up at the intrusive sound, as she gazed on the frosted glass of the aluminum door barely ten feet opposite her. Beyond it, she saw the silhouette of a big cowboy hat and little else. Something drew tight in her belly, and all her senses went on alert. She straightened, inhaled a few deep, fortifying breaths, and crossed to greet her—or rather, Sabrina's—visitor.

She gripped the doorknob carefully, inhaled again, then twisted and pushed slowly. But a gust of brutal wind snatched the door from her hand and sent it crashing outward, giving neither Rachel, nor her guest, a chance to ease slowly into things.

"Whoa," the cowboy hat said in response to the clatter of metal slapping against metal.

"Wow," Rachel gasped at the same time. Not because the wind had surprised her so, but because the cowboy hat tipped backward, and she got a good look at what was underneath.

Beautiful jumped into her head. He'd no doubt balk at being referred to in such a way, but that was the only word Rachel could come up with to describe him. His dark brown eyes were made darker still by the length of black hair that fell from beneath his Stetson, and by the two slashes of black eyebrows above and a ring of sooty lashes around each. His skin, too, was brown, a deep, smooth umber that was obviously a part of his heritage. His cheekbones were high and well-defined, his nose was straight and elegant, and they were complemented by a sensuously full lower lip that just begged to be tasted.

Oh, yeah. Definitely beautiful.

"Miss Jensen?" he said, sending a rush of heat right through her.

Shoot, heat was the last thing she needed, in spite of the frigid air buffeting her from all sides. When the man's voice finally registered in her muddled brain, she sensed by its tone that he must have uttered those two words several times without receiving an answer. Rachel shook her head, then forced herself to meet his gaze.

"Yes?" she replied, proud of herself for forming even that one-word response.

"Sabrina Jensen?"

A faint alarm bell sounded in the back of Rachel's head, and for a moment, she felt like the proverbial deer trapped in the headlights of an oncoming semi. It certainly wasn't the first time someone had thought she was Sabrina, nor would it be the last. Mistaken identity was something identical twins just had to live with. Normally, a brief, "Oh, no, I'm Sabrina's twin sister, Rachel," put a quick and painless end to the error.

But then, normally, Sabrina's questionable safety and recent bizarre behavior weren't an issue. Suddenly, with the up-in-the-air quality that Sabrina's life had adopted, Rachel's answer to the man's supposition now took on new importance.

She realized then that she had two options. One, she could correct him, as she invariably did when one of her sister's friends or acquaintances mistook her for her twin, and then she and the cowboy hat could share a chuckle.

That, of course, was assuming that this man was a friend or acquaintance, which he probably wasn't, if he was asking her if she was Sabrina Jensen. If Sabrina had met this particular cowboy hat during her brief stint in Wallace Canyon, he'd realize right off the bat that there was something different about Rachel. Namely, the fact that she clearly *wasn't* seven months pregnant. In a word, *duh.*

So if this cowboy, however beautiful, *wasn't* a friend or acquaintance of Sabrina's, well then he might just be anybody. And *any*body could be *some*body who wanted to do Sabrina harm. After all, Sabrina had told her that someone was after her. That the someone in question might be trying to take Sabrina's unborn child. Who knew who that someone might be? And he might not be working alone. It might just be a beautiful man with bitter-sweet chocolate eyes and a luscious lower lip.

Which brought Rachel to choice number two where mistaken identity was concerned.

She straightened, squared her shoulders and met those gorgeous brown eyes one-on-one. Then she told the man evenly, "Yes. I'm Sabrina Jensen. What can I do for you?"

* * *

The Sheriff and the Impostor Bride
will be on sale in December!

SILHOUETTE
DESIRE®

AVAILABLE FROM 19TH NOVEMBER 1999

The Perfect Fit Cait London

A TallChief Man of the Month

Nick Palladin refuses to marry Silver Tallchief just for the sake of a
business deal, but when she moves into his home and sends his
hormones haywire, suddenly he can't wait!

The Sheriff and the Impostor Bride Elizabeth Bevarly

Follow That Baby

Her pregnant twin was missing! Strapping sheriff Riley Hunter was
convinced she was the mum-to-be. Should she admit the truth?

His Ultimate Temptation Susan Crosby

An independent woman and an overprotective man, they'd loved but
parted as 'just friends'. Now trapped together their primitive desires are
irresistible…

Just a Little Bit Married? Eileen Wilks

Dark, brooding Raz Rasmussin had been hired to protect Sara Grace, so
they were posing as newlyweds, but they began to take the honeymoon
too seriously!

The Millionaire's Christmas Wish Shawna Delacorte

Millionaire Chance Fowler kissed a pretty stranger to dodge the press who
followed him. But then he couldn't forget her, so he had to find her…

Marriage, Outlaw Style Cindy Gerard

Outlaw Hearts

Waking up next to Clay James was absolutely crazy, even if he was
gorgeous and had come to her rescue. Suddenly, Maddie Brannigan was
in trouble—the 6lb 12oz kind!

9911

AVAILABLE FROM 19TH NOVEMBER 1999

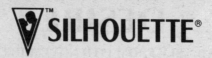

Sensation
A thrilling mix of passion, adventure and drama

CHRISTMAS LONE-STAR STYLE Linda Turner
IT CAME UPON A MIDNIGHT CLEAR Suzanne Brockmann
FOR CHRISTMAS, FOREVER Ruth Wind
HOME FOR CHRISTMAS Patricia Potter

Intrigue
Danger, deception and desire

ALL I WANT FOR CHRISTMAS Joanna Wayne
THE BEST-KEPT SECRET Adrianne Lee
DEAR SANTA Alice Orr
BRIDES OF THE NIGHT Maggie Shayne & Marilyn Tracy

Special Edition
Compelling romances packed with emotion

NATURAL BORN LAWMAN Sherryl Woods
WIFE IN THE MAIL Marie Ferrarella
BABY'S FIRST CHRISTMAS Cathy Gillen Thacker
THE SECRET DAUGHTER Jackie Merritt
THE ONLY COWBOY FOR CAITLIN Lois Faye Dyer
UNEXPECTED FAMILY Laurie Campbell

9911

FREE!

4 Books
and a surprise gift!

We would like to take this opportunity to thank you for reading this Silhouette® book by offering you the chance to take FOUR more specially selected titles from the Desire™ series absolutely FREE! We're also making this offer to introduce you to the benefits of the Reader Service™—

- ★ FREE home delivery
- ★ FREE gifts and competitions
- ★ FREE monthly Newsletter
- ★ Books available before they're in the shops
- ★ Exclusive Reader Service discounts

Accepting these FREE books and gift places you under no obligation to buy; you may cancel at any time, even after receiving your free shipment. Simply complete your details below and return the entire page to the address below. *You don't even need a stamp!*

YES! Please send me 4 free Desire books and a surprise gift. I understand that unless you hear from me, I will receive 6 superb new titles every month for just £2.70 each, postage and packing free. I am under no obligation to purchase any books and may cancel my subscription at any time. The free books and gift will be mine to keep in any case.

D9EB

Ms/Mrs/Miss/Mr ....Initials ....
BLOCK CAPITALS PLEASE

Surname ....

Address ....

....

....Postcode ....

Send this whole page to:
UK: The Reader Service, FREEPOST CN81, Croydon, CR9 3WZ
EIRE: The Reader Service, PO Box 4546, Kilcock, County Kildare (stamp required)

Offer not valid to current Reader Service subscribers to this series. We reserve the right to refuse an application and applicants must be aged 18 years or over. Only one application per household. Terms and prices subject to change without notice. Offer expires 31st May 2000. As a result of this application, you may receive further offers from Harlequin Mills & Boon Limited and other carefully selected companies. If you would prefer not to share in this opportunity please write to The Data Manager at the address above.

Silhouette is a registered trademark used under license.
Desire is being used as a trademark.

Celebrate Christmas with the Fortunes!

The incredibly popular
Fortune's Children series
returns with three new stories in:

A Fortune's Children™

CHRISTMAS

**At the company Christmas Party, Kate Fortune gives
three Fortune bachelors one year to fulfil a family
tradition and find wealth, power and everlasting
love. Find out if they are up to the challenge.**

On sale from 22nd October 1999